Calabrian Summer

Calabrian Summer

MARJORIE McEVOY

DOUBLEDAY & COMPANY, INC.

GARDEN CITY, NEW YORK

1980

For Felicity and Mark

All of the characters in this book
are fictitious, and any resemblance
to actual persons, living or dead,
is purely coincidental.

ISBN 0-385-15939-0
Library of Congress Catalog Card Number 79-6540
Copyright © 1980 by Marjorie McEvoy
All Rights Reserved
Printed in the United States of America
First Edition

Chapter One

They no longer deport men for stealing sheep in this wild region of Wales. Nor do they hang them for rustling their neighbor's stocky black cattle. Not in this second quarter of the twentieth century.

In other respects Nantallon has changed very little. The same sleepy fishing village clustering round the harbor. The same rugged castle perched high on the cliffs to the north. The same eternal hills.

Yet never again quite the same to me. Too much has happened this last year or so. Strange, dramatic events that changed me too suddenly from a wide-eyed teen-ager to a mature woman, having plumbed the depths and the heights.

I live in the castle. It has always been my home except for that brief, searing interlude in the wild mountains of Calabria. Now I shall never leave it again, not for the most luxurious dwelling that money could buy. Luxury does not bring happiness. All I want is for my love to join me here, in the rugged grandeur of Nantallon, where time stands still and life goes gently by.

So different from the gaunt, half-ruined castle frowning down from its heights in that desolate region of Southern Italy. Or from the Villa Caterina, beautiful, cold, impersonal, where I was born.

That, and my name, Lisa Moravia, brands me indisputably Italian. As does my raven-black hair and passionate, artistic nature. Yet Wales, and gray old Nantallon Castle, welcomed me as a tiny baby when my father rejected me, so, of course, it is where my heart will always be.

And in the grounds is Margaret's rose garden, where I always feel closest to her. How meticulously I tend it, as she used to do.

We were half sisters, but so close. The same mother, vivacious Megan Thomas, who captured Geraint Owen, the catch of the district, and was carried in triumph over the threshold of Nantallon Castle as his bride, thirty years ago. The hoped for son and heir never materialized though. Only Margaret, and when she was five years old, her father was thrown while riding in the hills, and killed.

Megan was stunned. After the first shock had worn off she left young Margaret with a nurse and began a leisurely tour of Europe to ease the restlessness that now beset her. Not romantic cities and fashionable resorts. They would have had little appeal for one brought up at Nantallon. No, she and her friend headed their hired car for unknown regions, as wild as the mountains of Wales.

So it was that they found themselves in Calabria, in the deep south of Italy, and there in Almina she met Pietro Moravia, who later became my father.

He was much older than she, a widower, and so charming, cultured, and friendly that they began to see each other frequently. When Megan's English lady friend was forced to return home, Megan, already deeply involved with Pietro, elected to stay on in Almina's one passable hotel. The outcome was predictable. They married and she went to live in his Villa Caterina, on the outskirts of the small hill town.

Margaret dimly remembered the excitement of being taken out there by her nurse. The childless Pietro made a great fuss of her, and she might have settled there, but for the fact that she was now ready for school. There were no good private English-speaking schools in the region, so she was sent back to Wales and spent only the holidays out in Italy.

"I loved the holidays," she used to tell me. "The villa had such exciting gardens with fountains and statues. Inside it was just as beautiful. Full of art treasures that Pietro had collected over the years. He was wealthy enough, with a substantial estate of bergamot groves, from which comes fragrant oil for perfume, and very fond of Megan. She was so happy with him that she didn't seem to miss Nantallon and Wales, or even me, her child, so you can imagine how delighted they were when presently Megan found she was pregnant.

"I was happy too at the idea of a little sister or brother," Margaret confessed. "I was nine years old then, and just developing a mothering instinct. It could have been just wonderful when you were born, if fate hadn't been so cruel in killing our mother in the process."

It was all so unexpected. A sudden complication, no advanced hospital at hand, and snow-bound mountain roads making it impossible for her to be moved. She died in the night in Pietro's arms, leaving me, Lisa, a wailing scrap of humanity in her place.

Perhaps it was little wonder that he turned against me, and could not bear to have me about the place. I could understand, and had long since forgiven him. He sent me to Nantallon in charge of a nurse, and built a hospital in memory of his dead wife.

Margaret made up for it. In spite of being only nine years older, she sort of mothered me, in gray Nantallon Castle, supplementing in devotion what my nurse gave me in practical care. She was fond of horses, and after finishing her education, started a riding school, a source of pleasure to me too, later on.

Yet, in spite of my Welsh upbringing my Italian origin asserted itself as I grew. My artistic nature found an outlet in painting and sketching. It became my star subject at school, and during my last year at boarding school, I spent all my spare time dreaming of becoming a second Constable.

It was during this last year that the devastating changes began, starting with that unexpected summons to Italy for Margaret. She was twenty-seven then and, oddly, had never married. Too busy with running her stables, Nantallon, and mothering me, perhaps.

We had neither of us ever been back to the Villa Caterina since I was banished, although a generous allowance had been regularly paid into an English bank for my upbringing. Then out of the blue came the message. Signor Pietro Moravia, now sixty-three, was gravely ill and wanted to see us both.

How strangely things turn out. There happened to be an epidemic of scarlet fever at my school that winter and I was one of the victims. So, of course, I was incarcerated in the sick bay, and Margaret had to rush off without me.

"I'll be back before you're up and about again," she declared, but in that she was too optimistic. Pietro Moravia, my unknown father, died and was buried while I was still covered with an itchy red rash. She wrote that she would have to stay on at the villa to settle his affairs with the lawyers, but that I could join her later.

Again it was not to be. When I at last left quarantine I had a lot of studying and exams to catch up on. It was still only half term. "You can come out in the Easter holidays," Margaret wrote. "You'll be finished school then, and we can stay on here for a lengthy holiday, since the villa and all its contents now belongs to me."

Perhaps the old prejudice against me had never died. At all events, my father had left the entire estate to Margaret and merely a considerable sum of money to me.

I was not in the least jealous. We had always shared things, so it would make little difference which of us owned the place, I reasoned. The intriguing thing was that we now possessed an Italian estate. What fun we could have, now that I was eighteen, about to finish with school, and would soon be my own mistress. Italy was a paradise for artists, it was said. My painting and sketching should blossom into something worthwhile out there.

So the shock was devastating when, just a few days before I was due to leave school, the letter came. A brief, scrappy letter from Margaret, telling me she was to be married the following day.

Don't be hurt darling. I wanted more than anything to have you here as a bridesmaid, but it has all been too sudden to arrange anything like that. In any case, having buried my step-father so recently, for decency's sake the ceremony has to be absolutely private and quiet.

Poor Lisa. Never having even heard the name of Enrico Gorini, this must all come as a shock to you. Indeed, the suddenness of it all leaves even me breathless. I thought I was destined to be a spinster all my life, but Enrico changed all that. He has been manager of the bergamot groves belonging to the Villa Caterina this last year or two, so I met him soon after arriving here, and he has proved a tower of strength to me in my ordeal. Such a man! Such strength of character! How could a Welsh country mouse like me, resist him! But, of course, you will see him for yourself soon, I hope. For the next month we shall be touring Rome and the northern art cities. After that we'll make arrangements for you to join us out here for a holiday at least. I haven't a clue how we'll arrange the future, yours and Nantallon's, but there's all the time in the world to work things out. In any case, you're so pretty that you're sure to marry much earlier than I did. In the meantime, have a lazy Easter at Nantallon. Invite one of your school friends to stay with you and keep you company.

The letter dropped from my hand. I just plopped down on my dormitory bed and sat hunched there in silent misery.

Margaret had betrayed me, I thought bitterly. Having never taken much interest in any man to date, I never dreamed of her taking the plunge at long last. Least of all in such a hurried fashion, to someone I'd never heard of, in an outlandish hill town of Italy that would cut us off from each other in the most fiendish way.

For how could things ever be the same between us? If I joined her at the villa, I should now feel an intruder between her and this Enrico, probably some impossible peasant upstart, who had worked his way up in Pietro's service, and then inveigled Margaret into marrying him, for the sake of the estate that now went with her.

The estate, that but for a fiendish trick of fate, should have been mine. I was Pietro's daughter, born in the shuttered master bedroom of the villa I could not remember, while Margaret was as Welsh as Nantallon.

The last few days at school were a nightmare, endured in silent misery. My friends had their own plans, and I parted without a word of my personal problems to anyone, on that windy March day.

But how sickeningly silent Nantallon seemed with no cheerful Margaret to greet me and talk over future plans. Only the middle-aged couple and their daughter who lived in and ran the place, after a fashion. Half the rooms were permanently closed and sheeted. Now the remainder might just as well be the same, for all the life there was around, I reflected.

Art proved my salvation. I turned to it with a hungry desperation, roaming the countryside for material, sketching and painting for dear life. I would make Margaret proud of me one day, I vowed. By the time she sent for me, I should be accomplished enough to put it first, not really caring that I had been supplanted in her affections.

March and April passed. Now she should be back at the villa, I reflected, as the warmer weather of May filled Nantallon village with trippers and caravaners, down for the fishing and the sailing. No doubt she was changing things a little. Adding a few new furnishings to replace the faded brocades left by an old man. Setting her personal seal on the place as most brides would naturally do.

Then, when all was to her liking, she would summon me to go out to them.

I wrote once, but received no reply. I think this hurt even more than Margaret's marriage. This unknown Enrico must have really bewitched her if all she felt for me now was indifference.

Then, about the middle of May, the oddest message arrived. It was in Margaret's handwriting, but such a shaky scrawl that I could scarcely decipher it. When I did manage to make sense of it, it sent a cold shiver down my spine.

Good-bye, darling Lisa. I just had to say it while I can still hold a pen. I know I shall never see you again, and the happy times we planned together out here can never be. It is too late for regrets now. Make your home permanently at our beloved Nantallon, which I leave to you, and forget Italy if you value your happiness. There seems to be a curse on the villa.

Your loving Margaret

If I had been depressed before, I was now frantic. It needed little perception to see that she felt she was dying. Margaret, as strong and healthy as the agile Welsh sheep when she went out there. What on earth could have happened to her to bring about such a drastic change in so short a time?

Well, I could soon find out. How should I ever forgive myself if I dithered around until action was useless. I must get out to her, see for myself what was wrong and try to persuade her to return to Nantallon with me. Perhaps the searing heat of Southern Italy in summer did not suit a person used to the bracing mountain air of Wales. Surely her husband would agree to any measures if his wife's health, even her life, were at stake.

Feverishly I began to make preparations.

Traveling on the Continent was not easy, now that we had been at war with Germany for seven months. Here in rural Wales it affected us little. We had plenty of home-grown food, and our little fishing community went on much as before. Further afield things were slowly deteriorating. The splendid night ferry train from London to Paris had been withdrawn, Margaret had discovered when she had tried to book earlier in the year. It was still possible to travel through France to Italy if one had a valid reason, but troops and supplies had priority, and punctuality was a thing of the past.

Well, if she could do it, so could I. By pulling a few strings with friends who mattered, I managed to book trains and sleepers for the first week in June then set about packing a case that I could manage to transport myself in foreign stations.

With the brashness of youth, I felt supremely confident that I should encounter no insurmountable difficulties in reaching Calabria and inducing Margaret and her husband to return with me to Wales, for it was hardly likely that she would be willing to part from him, or he allow his recent bride to travel so far away without him. The thought of a stranger at Nantallon, of sharing our home and Margaret and everything we loved was distinctly unpalatable, but better that than leaving her to pine away in a place that did not seem to agree with her.

The day before departure arrived. I rose early, tense and restless, wishing it was time to go, for how could I settle to anything under the circumstances. Breakfast, cooked as usual by our efficient couple, had to be forced down, and I was glad when the morning post arrived to create a diversion.

And what a diversion! There was one letter from Italy that I clutched with a terrific lurch of the heart, then sped to the morning room to read in privacy.

The sheet of paper that emerged when I tore open the envelope was a bitter disappointment. It bore the Villa Caterina address, but instead of Margaret's clear, rather schoolgirlish script, was written in bold heavy scrawl and signed Enrico Gorini. With dread in my heart I began to read:

Dear Lisa,

I feel free to address you in such intimate fashion, for after Margaret's frequent reference to you, I consider you a distant relative. It is all the more distasteful then that my first contact with you should be in such painful circumstances.

I am a man of direct approach, so will come to the point, which is that I have the most distressing news for you concerning Margaret. Unhappily, she is no longer with us. Cholera is no stranger to this part of Italy. An epidemic descended on Almina and carried off a number of unfortunates, including my poor bride.

Your shock and grief must be as great as my own, so what can I say? Nothing, except that time will heal.

In accordance with the custom locally, the villa and estate now belong legally to me. This will not be any real deprivation to you, as with no previous contact, the place can mean nothing to you. Also you have Nantallon Castle and an adequate income, so I feel no qualms about the situation.

Rest assured, a suitable marble monument will be erected to your stepsister's memory. Everything possible was done to save her, but like other victims, she quickly succumbed.

If there is any keepsake of hers you would care to have, name it and I will send it. There is no point in your attempting the tedious journey out to Almina. Travel across France is difficult and slow, owing to the war with Germany, and you are too young and vulnerable to attempt it, especially with nothing at the end of it.

So, with deepest condolences,

Enrico Gorini

The note paper fluttered from my shaking hand. Oh, the numbing horror of it! Never again to see my dear, kind Margaret, or experience the delights of the villa and its gardens under her proud ownership.

It was too late for all that.

Too late to help the only person I had ever truly loved.

Chapter Two

How long I would have crouched there, too stunned and helpless to think or move, I don't know. The entrance of Beth to
dust and tidy up, and her kindly concern, drove me out. I could
not bring myself to tell her the terrible news just yet.

The fresh air and movement revived me a little. Reason began to function again and with it, vague doubts and suspicions.
Enrico's letter seemed genuine enough, but what of that odd
disturbing letter I had earlier received from Margaret? Over a
fortnight ago, in fact, so it must have been written nearly a
month ago, allowing for the time it would take to arrive in these
war disrupted times.

She couldn't possibly have been suffering from cholera then.
It was a disease that struck swiftly and developed like wildfire.
So what lay behind that strange epistle? Of what had she been
afraid?

It needed probing into, I concluded, and with the arrogance
of youth, felt that I was the only one to do it. All arrangements
had been made for the journey. I would let them stand, in spite
of Enrico's assumption that the journey was too hazardous for
a girl of eighteen.

Yes, I would go out and surprise him. Perhaps uncover more
than lay on the surface. Anything but stay here, alone and un-
happy.

In my state of feverish impatience, the day seemed never ending, and the night that followed, full of bad dreams. In between
I lay brooding.

Was the Villa Caterina under some evil spell? Were all
brides who entered there doomed to sudden death? The last

two had certainly both perished within a brief spell. First my mother, and now my half sister. Was I myself fortunate in never having set foot in the place since leaving it in my nurse's arms? Well, I should soon find out.

I looked pale and haggard when I rose in the early hours to catch the milk train to Cardiff. At the last moment an odd disinclination to leave Nantallon gripped me. I shrugged it off as nerves, walked the short distance to the windswept halt by the sea, and chugged my slow way to the frequent clashing of milk churns.

The express from Cardiff to Paddington was crowded. Only now did the full realization that we were at war strike me. So many fresh-faced young men in khaki leaving for destinations unknown. For the first time a twinge of misgiving assailed me. Would I find the journey more difficult than I had imagined? Well, difficult or not, it had to be undertaken even if I died in the attempt.

London seemed reassuringly normal in the sunshine of a late spring afternoon, apart from the gas masks in evidence, the barrage balloons above, and the absence of children, long since evacuated. I crowded onto the top deck of a bus, and watched the city unfold about me as it trundled me slowly, with stops and changes, across to Victoria Station.

How fearfully busy the station was, dispatching troops and equipment across to France. Sinister overtones loomed in the shape of posters. "Careless talk costs lives," and "Is your journey really necessary?" blazoned forth from posters everywhere. Well, mine was for my own peace of mind.

I was allowed to board a train for Dover eventually and found myself squeezed in between a burly Cockney sergeant and a girl in naval uniform. She made the tedious journey bearable by sharing her sandwiches and a flask of tea with me, neither of which I had thought necessary to bring along.

"You'd better get yourself organized if you're going all the way to Southern Italy," she advised after we had opened up to each other. "One can't rely on getting anything these days, not even trains on time."

Her kindly common sense reminded me painfully of Margaret. What a sheltered life I had led, I now realized, spent mainly in the cloistered care of a girls' school, and the wild remoteness of rural Wales. What did I know of the world? Had I been an impetuous little fool to rush off in such uncertain times instead of waiting and consulting the family solicitor?

Well the die was cast now. I was on my way, and nothing would deter me.

The night was spent at a dingy little hotel near the docks, since my boat did not leave until the following morning. Then this proved to be even more crowded than the trains had been. All the cabin seats were taken, which forced me out on deck in the cold sea mist.

I was glad to leave the boat behind at Calais, but conditions there were equally trying. There was a two-hour wait before I could board a train for Paris, and the war-time lunch of soup and an omelette was not at all satisfying.

Conditions on the Paris Express were appalling. I had to fight my way on, and then stand in the corridor for the whole of the journey. It was a very weary me who climbed down at the Gare du Nord.

From there I must cross to Gare Lyon for the Rome Express. Fortunately, it would not leave before evening, so I was not harassed by time in addition to other discomforts.

Since courage failed at the prospect of the Metro, with its unknown hazards, I at last managed to bag a decrepit taxi, shared with three other people, to jerk and jostle us across the city, no longer gay, even in early June. The realities of a nation at war were more obvious here than in London.

Then a further wait at the crowded southern station. I managed to obtain a meal of sorts, and in addition, bought a picnic box and a bottle of vin rouge to take with me as a precaution. I also managed to change the bulk of my money into Italian lire.

The Rome Express was late. What if it should not arrive at all and a dreary night on a hard station bench lay ahead of me? I thought in a panic. But at last it materialized, and I was aboard and being shown to my couchette by the uniformed attendant, a dragon-faced female who snapped out unintelligible orders in French. Neither my French nor Italian had got very far at school.

I stared round the confined space in stupefied dismay. Six couchettes in two tiers of three confronted me. This compartment would be my home for the next twenty-four hours, I realized with a grimace, but of course there would be more space tomorrow, when the attendant stowed away the berths.

Absolute bedlam took over for the next fifteen minutes. The corridors were jammed with passengers and luggage, many of them in uniform, demanding in half a dozen languages their seats, their couchettes, their sleepers. I had nowhere to sit and could not retire to my top bunk until the commotion ceased and my fellow travelers made their appearance.

They arrived eventually. Not the party of stout matrons I had envisaged, but a middle-aged couple with three giggling daughters.

With a shriek and a jolt we were off, to thunder through the night toward Italy and the unknown.

The family began disrobing, filling the claustrophobic space to suffocation. As I could see no washing facilities and the corridor was now clear, I decided to look for a toilet compartment and give this lot a chance to retire in privacy.

Lurching and bumping along the narrow corridor, I found what I sought and made my ablutions. It was more difficult returning. Passengers were coming and going, and the train swayed more than ever as it gathered speed for its long journey.

Perhaps I was tired after my fatiguing day. Whatever the cause, I lost my balance as we thundered over some points, to land squarely in the arms of a hefty male coming my way. And what a figure of a man. Tall, broad, with deeply tanned face, eyes like sloes, and hair just as glossily black above them.

A torrent of words rushed from him, the only one of which I understood being *signorina*. How I wished I had worked harder during those foreign language sessions at school. The few phrases I recalled seemed woefully inadequate now.

"I'm English," I explained in embarrassment, recalling the warnings I had heard regarding Latin males, and hastily apologized for my clumsiness. My attempt to extricate myself from his hold was not successful.

"Then we shall speak English," he declared, in a surprisingly good rendering of it, "although you look Italian. Where is your sleeper?"

"A good deal farther on, signore, and it's a crowded couchette. I'd better get back before they drop off to sleep, since I'm certain to have to climb up to the top bunk."

He laughed. "Let them wait. This is too uncivilized an hour to retire. If you have nowhere to sit, you are welcome to share my first-class compartment until you really wish to sleep."

Here we go, I thought. What did he take me for?

My hasty refusal only made him smile.

"So you think me a wolf who would gobble you up? You are wrong. My compartment is shared with another. A fat Frenchman who speaks not a word of any other language. All he does is drink cognac and read his newspaper. A confoundedly dull fellow. You would do me a favor to join me over coffee, which I have just ordered. I'm not partial to my own company."

"Coffee?" It sounded heavenly. "If you'll tell me where it can be had, I'll order some myself," I added, caution prevailing.

He shook his head. "Too late, signorina. The supply is strictly limited these days. They serve only the first-class passengers. Now come and sit down. Here is my compartment, and there, see, is the fat Frenchman, a truly formidable chaperone."

After a swift glance for confirmation, I weakly gave in. What harm could come to me with such a specimen of fatherly respectability sitting opposite.

This individual, after a hostile glare at the pair of us, returned to his newspaper. I began to side with my new acquaintance.

He neither volunteered his name, nor asked mine, only how long I would be staying in Rome.

"Merely until I can catch a connection to the south," I said, determined to keep the conversation facile and my private business to myself.

"That won't be immediately, signorina, with the tourist season in full swing. You will be forced to stay overnight at least."

The coffee now made its appearance. Not just a cup slopping over into the saucer but a tray complete with coffee pot, separate milk and cup.

How had he managed to command such luxury, I wondered, as he snapped out an order for a second cup which was promptly obeyed. By a superlative tip, or sheer personality?

The beverage was much better than any I had tasted recently. I drank it gratefully then insisted that I must now find my own sleeping quarters.

He shrugged. "So! You do not intend to sing for your supper, so to speak? No matter! Away with you. We shall no doubt bump into each other again tomorrow."

Was he laughing at me, or piqued because I declined to linger? It was impossible to say. But his bold black eyes, raking lazily over me as he swung open the door for me to pass, made me suddenly glad of the Frenchman's presence.

By accident or design, I saw little of him the following day as we hurtled south. The family with whom I was incarcerated soon accepted me as one of themselves, thrusting their warm Italian hospitality upon me. Their stores of food and drink seemed inexhaustible, all of which was at my disposal as soon as my own had been consumed. Perhaps it was my Italian name and appearance, or my youthful unworldliness, but whatever it was, the plump mama insisted on mothering me like one of her own daughters.

"You must spend the night under our roof as we live on the outskirts of Rome, little Lisa," she declared in a mixture of Italian and English, on learning that I must change trains there for Paola. "It is not good for one so young and pretty to wander alone, looking for a vacant room. The hotels are very busy at this time of year, and in Rome as in other cities there are unscrupulous people on the lookout for such as you."

"*Grazie, signora*," I said with sincerity, glad of such kindly help, now that my initial bravado was wearing thin.

I did catch another glimpse of the first-class passenger as we jostled into the taxi queue at Roma Termini, burdened with our luggage. He was just ahead of us, coolly competent, a servile porter carrying his case. As he imperiously hailed a vehicle he nonchalantly ordered, "Grand Hotel, Corso Porta Nuova," then, in turning to tip the porter, his glance fell upon me.

He took in the situation immediately, me safely in the bosom of a gregarious family. Then raising his hat in exaggerated salute, he boarded the taxi and was gone.

"Grand Hotel!" the eldest girl exclaimed. "He must be a millionaire, *mama, mia.*"

"And appears to know signorina Lisa," Mama said with lively curiosity.

Embarrassed, I was glad that our own taxi materialized at that moment, and I was saved an explanation.

The ensuing night was pleasant enough, and next morning the plump signora hired a *carrozza* to transport me to the railway station, so that I might see some of the sights of Rome in passing. I was genuinely sorry to wave *arrivederci* to these kindly people.

But the city unfurling about me as the horse clip-clopped along, captured my interest immediately. How different it was from rural Wales. The sparkling fountains, the brown-robed priests, the school children with their little blue overalls and white neck bows, the orange trees bearing both fragrant blossom and mature fruit. And overhead the sun shining with a brilliance unknown back home.

The station was as noisy and crowded as yesterday, but I had no difficulty in finding a seat on the Paola express, with my pre-booked reservation. And this journey would be short and simple after my last ordeal. A mere four hours. I should be in Paola by lunch time.

The bustle and stress of travel had driven the melancholy reason for its necessity to the back of my mind, but on reaching Paola it pressed in on me again. For now I must make my way into the interior. The wild and brooding mountains of Calabria, where tourists seldom ventured and life for the peasants was grindingly hard. Only a few aristocrats were wealthy and powerful, like my late father.

Now, with a jolt, the reality of my birth came home to me. Whether I liked it or not, I was a legitimate daughter of this unknown region of Italy, however strongly I thought of myself as British.

It was ironical really. But for a trick of fate I should have been queening it at the Villa Caterina, instead of coming here as a stranger and a supplicant begging for a few of Margaret's possessions.

I was by this time heartily sick of travel. Another wait would have been intolerable. Fortunately, by dispensing with lunch, I was just able to catch one of the infrequent trains that meandered up into the mountains to Cosenza, stopping at some of the hill towns on the way. Among these should be Almina, my destination.

How slowly we moved, the fussy little steam engine winding its tortuous way through tunnels and round hairpin bends, past hill villages drowsing in the afternoon sun, past great masses of golden broom, into the misty clouds at the highest points. Stopping places were few and far between, their stations open to the skies and boasting nothing so civilized as buffets. Barefooted, ragged urchins ran up and down the platform looking for baggage to carry, and a few shawled women in dingy-black were the only passengers.

Mercifully, the air was cooler up here, but the farther we traveled, the wilder grew the landscape about us. The soft green Welsh hillsides seemed tame by comparison with these harsh ridges and dramatic ravines through which ran watercourses, now almost dry.

Then suddenly, at last we reached Almina.

My heart beating fast, I clutched my case and stepped down onto the platform.

By heaven, in what desolate outpost had I landed myself? I thought in dismay, gazing at the weed-grown tracks, broken platforms, paint-peeling buildings, and trio of rusting steam engines huddled on a side line, quietly crumbling away. And beyond, the vast barren landscape frowning down upon it.

But where was the town?

An about-turn disclosed a huddle of off-white, flat-topped houses spilling down from a less-sheer hillside, and dominating all, on the very crest of the hill, a gaunt half-ruined castle that looked as though it had sprouted there from the rocks many centuries ago.

"*Carrozza, signorina?*"

It was a uniformed individual who combined the offices of ticket collector and porter.

"*Si, si!*" I said, not having the remotest idea of where the Villa Caterina lay, nor how far off.

The porter seized my case and ambled out to where a bony horse between the shafts of a dilapidated carriage, cropped what parched grass it could find.

The owner, dozing in the driving seat, jerked awake and leaped down at our approach.

"Villa Caterina?" I said without embellishment, doubtful if he would understand English.

"Villa Caterina?" An odd change came over the cheerful faces. A calculating wariness that made me uneasy.

"It is not far? Your horse can manage it?" I hoped they could at least understand the gist of what I said.

"*Si, si, signorina.*" The *carrozza* owner, servilely deferential now, seized my case and thrust it in, then handed me up beside it.

With a crack of the whip and a flurry of dust we were off, but the movement brought no exhilaration to me. An unformed dread had descended upon me. I was suddenly scared of this unknown land, and the ménage, where my two closest kinswomen had died so suddenly and tragically. If there was an evil spell on the place, might it not overshadow me too?

Now, when it was too late, I fervently wished I had not come.

Chapter Three

A river, now almost dry, ran past the station. We crossed the iron bridge that spanned it and began to ascend the main street through the town.

At close quarters it was dirty, untidy, and crowded with people emerging from the siesta to buy at the dark little shops that spilled out their wares onto the pavements. The side alleys opening off were narrow warrens of tall stone dwellings that shut out the sun and looked dankly noisome, the steeper ones ending in flights of broken steps. Crumbling, stucco churches reared themselves here and there, round which ragged urchins played, and everywhere was an air of apathy and neglect.

The town petered out. Now I could see the castle more clearly above. It carried the same air of decay in its fallen gray stones, and in addition, a sort of brooding menace.

Instead of taking the narrower road up that forked off to it, we bore left and continued along a country road to come upon, surprisingly enough, a large white building in comparatively good repair.

"Hospital, signorina," my driver explained. And then my heart jolted, for beside the great gates was an inscription. Though written in Italian, the names leaped out at me sufficiently familiarly to follow the gist of it.

"Founded in nineteen twenty-four by Signor Pietro Moravia, as a memorial to his wife, Megan, who died in childbirth."

My birth. My mother. My father. Suddenly this hostile land became less alien. I was part of it, and it of me. I pictured my grief-stricken father, those eighteen years ago, blaming this remote spot for my mother's death, because no modern facilities or highly skilled help had been available when needed quickly. Vowing to make amends by spending some of his wealth on a badly needed hospital, to help others in dire need, and my heart warmed to him, in spite of his coldness toward me.

Just past the hospital the road ran through a plantation of conifers, welcome shade after the glare of the sun. We emerged from this to find ourselves in another world. A world of silence, peace, and beauty, in sharp contrast to the activity and squalor of the town below.

On one side was open country, all massed yellow gorse among tall cypress trees and flowering shrubs. On the other, an extensive garden behind its sheltering wall.

And then came a great iron gate, fast shut as though to keep out uninvited guests.

"The Villa Caterina," my driver said, as he climbed down and handed out first my case and then me.

I paid the few lire he asked for and watched him go with a sinking inside me. What if I couldn't gain entry, and was marooned up here on my own?

But to my relief, I found the small side gate unlocked, and once inside, breathed more freely as I walked up the neglected drive to the villa.

As I reached it, the sound of a tolling bell in one of the crumbling churches below stole softly up, slow and solemn. A knell for dear dead Margaret, or a warning to me to go no farther?

The villa itself offered no more welcome than a tomb. Its great white-marble facade looked cold and dead, aided by the blank windows all shuttered in dark green. Life-size statues stood around on pedestals, their sightless eyes fixed upon me with unnerving concentration.

With reluctance I tugged on the bell rope that hung by the door, to hear a jangling within in response. It was like trying to raise the dead, for all the answer that came. I tugged again, and this time the result was more than I had bargained for. A sleek black dog of uncertain breed came bounding up and with snarls of rage, grabbed the left cuff of my light coat, its fangs nipping my wrist in the process.

As I cried out in pain and alarm, I heard a key being turned ponderously in the lock. The great door swung open and there stood a most unprepossessing individual. Thick set, bull-necked, with cold black eyes and dour expression, he gazed at me with the deepest suspicion.

"I came to see Signor Gorini," I said faintly, hoping desperately that he understood English. "Is this the kind of reception you give your visitors?"

"Signor Gorini is away on business," he said in accentuated English. "He has lately been bereaved and is receiving no one. Besides, you are a stranger. Go away, before the dog does you further harm."

"Why you surly lout!" I exclaimed, my mettle up now. "I'm a connection by marriage of your master's, was born in this villa, and have come all the way from Wales to see him. I'll not be put off so shabbily. Besides, my wrist needs attention."

I drew back my cuff and thrust it out. Scarlet blobs were welling up from the punctures inflicted.

"Best get along to the hospital," he said with complete indifference. "My orders are to admit no one."

With that he dragged the dog inside and slammed the door in my face.

This was beyond anything I had imagined. I certainly didn't intend to go tamely back to England without setting foot in the place, but for the moment I was defeated. Without prompt attention I could end up with blood poisoning or even rabies from that savage brute. There was no other course than to retrace my steps to the white building I had recently passed. Fortunately, it was not too far away, for I should have to carry my case.

I picked it up after fixing my handkerchief round the injury and trudged away, shocked and bewildered.

This was an entirely different aspect of the Villa Caterina from the pictures painted by Margaret. The captivating gardens she had adored on childish visits, the charm she had found on her recent return here. If it had all vanished with the death of my father, why had she been so enamored of the place that she had married the estate manager with the intention of remaining there for the rest of her days.

Enrico Gorini must hold the key to the answer, I reasoned. His attraction and personality must be truly outstanding to capture the staid Margaret in so brief a time.

At all costs I must hang on in Almina until he returned. The surly servant and belligerent hound had given me a poor and possibly false impression. No doubt things would take on a new perspective if I could talk with the new master.

Yes, I should call again when he returned.

The hospital now materialized, a welcome sight after the deep gloom of the copse, now that the light was fading. Pray heaven I should find the staff more sympathetic than the man I had just left. They might even help me to find shelter for the night.

The open door led into a reception hall, cool and clean, with benches round the walls, a fountain playing in the center, and a desk at one end. The receptionist sitting behind it was middle-aged, cosy, and kindly looking. She encouraged my hesitant entry with a smile and asked in Italian what she could do for me.

"I speak mainly English, in spite of my looks," I explained.

"So, then we shall converse in English. As our head doctor is from England, we have all picked up a little. Now what is your trouble?"

I held out my hand, letting the handkerchief fall from the wrist. "Do you have a casualty department I wonder? I have just been bitten by a dog."

She held up her hands in horror.

"But that is bad, signorina! And I'm sorry to say our outpatients department is now closed for the day. We are very short of doctors in this isolated outpost, but you ought to have treatment. Perhaps one of our nurses could help. I will ring through to the surgical ward."

She lifted the internal telephone, but before she could dial, a door opened and out came a man in a white coat. He was in his mid-thirties, with shrewd hazel eyes, a thoughtful expression, and straight fair hair that proclaimed him English. He set down a sheaf of papers on the desk then glanced at me.

"Ah, Dr. Crossley," the receptionist said. "I am in a quandary. Here is a young English girl who has been bitten by a dog. Is there anyone on duty who can attend to her?"

"English! We see few of those in Almina." His glance became more interested and then he took my hand and looked at the bleeding punctures.

"I shall attend to you myself, signorina, since dog bites could be dangerous if neglected," he said. "Please follow me."

"You'll be all right now, signorina," the receptionist said as I turned away. "That is our chief." The pride and confidence in her tone was reassuring.

At last fortune seemed to be with me. I followed him into what was evidently the casualty surgery and sat down while he disinfected the wound, explaining that it was not worth calling a nurse from the ward for such a brief session.

"Now I must cauterize it," he went on. "You'll feel a little pain, but not very bad. Afterward there'll be a tiny scar, but nothing to embarrass you."

I winced when the searing instrument touched me, but it was over in a moment.

He smiled encouragingly. "Good girl. Now a single prick with a hypodermic needle and it's over. Rabies, among other things, is endemic in these parts. We'll take no risks."

This, too, was soon over. By this time, I felt a little queasy and probably looked white around the gills, for he said, "Now I guess a cup of tea wouldn't come amiss. I've trained Signora Monisi, our receptionist, to make a really good English brew. Perhaps she'll oblige now."

He spoke into the desk phone, then looked at me with frank curiosity.

"Now perhaps I'm entitled to ask your name and how you managed to fall foul of a dog in such an isolated spot. Are you visiting Almina, Miss . . ."

"Lisa Moravia," I prompted. "A real Italian name isn't it? I guess that confuses you even more. Strictly speaking, I *am* Italian by birth, though having lived all my life in Wales, I consider myself British."

"Lisa Moravia!" He looked astounded. "You don't mean you are the banished daughter of Pietro Moravia, the founder of this hospital? The child who cost a mother's life?"

I nodded. "I was born in the Villa Caterina, but have never set eyes on it until today. And judging by my reception there when I called earlier, I'm as unwelcome now as I was then. A surly retainer and a savage dog were my greeting, Dr. Crossley."

His mouth hardened. "I can well imagine it. Things have changed drastically since Signor Moravia's death. I was his doctor and friend you know—a frequent visitor there when he was alive. The regime was gracious enough in his time. Then, when the estate passed to his stepdaughter, things altered. Enrico Gorini, the estate manager, married her soon after she came out to the villa. He dismissed the old trusted servants and appointed a few new ones. I've never been summoned there since, not even when his new wife was taken sick. There was a cholera outbreak at the time. I was rushed off my feet, both inside and outside the hospital, so it was a relief, really, when he summoned a doctor from Paola to stay at the villa and treat her. It didn't do the slightest good though. The victim died with the suddenness common to cholera."

"What diabolical luck," I said sadly, "to come to such an end! If only she'd stayed in Wales where she belonged. Is cholera painful? I hope she didn't suffer. Poor Margaret."

"Since I never saw the case, or even met the lady previously, I'm afraid I can tell you nothing."

He spoke slowly, with reservation. Was he keeping something back?

"I suppose it really *was* cholera that killed her?" I asked as a shot in the dark, recalling that strange resigned letter of Margaret's.

He spread his hands wide in a wholly Italian gesture.

"My dear Miss Moravia, who am I to cast doubts on the matter under the circumstances? Especially as this hospital functions chiefly on the grants received from the Villa Caterina estate. Your good-hearted father endowed it with a permanent legacy. The local authorities would never have bestirred themselves to build and maintain it from public funds. This is the poverty-stricken, neglected deep south you know. The poor relation of the more prosperous north."

I nodded. "Well, Dr. Crossley, I hope the town at least boasts a hotel of some sort, for I mean to hang on here until I manage to beard the lion in his den and hear more about Margaret's end. Fortunately, the road runs downhill. I shouldn't fancy carrying my case up."

"There's no need to carry it anywhere this evening, especially as it is now almost dark," he said decisively. "Fortunately we have a spare room, now that the epidemic is over. You are a patient, after all, and I consider a second injection wise. You will have that tomorrow morning and then there should be no unpleasant aftermath."

I colored with gratitude. "How very kind you are, Doctor. It *would* have been an ordeal, trudging around in the dark in a strange foreign town where probably few speak English, and I very little Italian."

"Especially Almina, signorina."

"Now you must explain that cryptic remark."

He shrugged. "It is a strange, in some ways sinister place. A stronghold of the Mafia for decades, though with the conspiracy of silence, no one can ever pin them down or obtain sufficient evidence for convictions. Murders are commonplace, and extortion more so. I suspect I have only been allowed to reign here these past years by keeping myself strictly neutral, my mouth and ears closed, and my clinic ever open to violent injuries with no questions asked. Otherwise, some dark night while on my way to an emergency I'd have been waylaid and exterminated before this, no doubt, especially now that my patron, Signor Moravia, is dead."

My eyes widened, but recalling my reception at the villa, I was forced to believe him.

"Oh, I didn't mean to alarm you," he added hastily. "It's all subversive, and on a short visit, you shouldn't be aware of it at all. Now I'll ring for an orderly to show you to your room, and then perhaps you would take dinner with us in the senior staff dining room? We eat in five minutes."

"How kind of you, Doctor."

The room was small, plain, but adequate to my needs. I flung off my coat, freshened my face and followed the orderly to a larger but no less austere room with a center dining table.

Apart from Dr. Crossley, the seniors were all Italian, but they made me welcome in the warm-hearted Latin way and spoke partly in English in deference to me. Through the conversation I gathered that a new menace had fallen on this country. Fascism was rampant under the dictator, Mussolini, and the shadow of war loomed nearer for them, too, as this violent regime openly allied itself to the notorious Hitler. However, this did not trouble me in the least. Even our own open warfare with Germany had affected me very little as yet.

I retired early and slept deeply after my days of travel, feeling safe and secure in this little sterile world tucked away in the hills. Breakfast was brought to me in my room, after which I saw Dr. Crossley briefly for my second injection.

How nice he was, I thought, and so English with his straight fair hair, hazel eyes, and tall slim figure. To me, at eighteen, he seemed almost fatherly in his mid-thirties. Back home he would probably have been married these past ten years, with a growing family to harass and interest him. Here in this wilderness he no doubt made the hospital his world, having little scope to find a mate among this largely illiterate peasant population.

"There's one passable pensione in Almina on the Via Santa Rosa," he told me. "You might weather a brief stay there, but my advice, for what it is worth, is to forget the Villa Caterina and go straight back to your homely Wales. So far, you've had no cause to love the place. It's brought nothing but trouble to you and your folk. Now, under the new regime, I can't see any change except for the worse. Enrico Gorini is in complete possession now, I believe. A man held in some awe round here. What do you hope to achieve by seeing him, since what is past can't be recalled?"

My mouth took on a stubborn line.

"Could *you* resist such a challenge, Dr. Crossley? Come so far and not force an entrance to the house where you were born, to take a last look? To find out what so fascinated Margaret about the place and Gorini that she was bowled over in such a short time."

He laughed suddenly, and now he looked more boyish.

"Sure I couldn't. Only take care. And remember, the hospital is close by if you care to call in before you return to Wales. Now I must fly or I'll never get through my morning's work."

His handclasp was warm, firm, and so reassuring. I clung to him in a panic for a moment. It was almost like leaving a bit of home behind as I walked out through the mosaic floored hall, its benches now lined with drab, patient-looking humanity, and trudged down the hill.

The half-ruined castle crowning it looked dark and somber when I glanced upward. Like an eagle in its aerie ready to swoop on some unsuspecting prey. What a marvelous subject for a sketch, I thought. I must try to climb up and take a closer look before I left Almina.

Head down, deep in thought, I scarcely heard the expensive engine of the opulent car that came purring up the hill. Not until it was almost upon me and startled me with a blast on the horn that sent me leaping to the side of the track.

The next moment I was even more startled. Convinced that it must be a wealthy patient with sudden illness in a hurry to reach the hospital, I stared at the man gripping the steering wheel, an attractive woman by his side.

It was none other than the stranger of the train journey who had shared his coffee with me. He certainly recognized me too, I knew instinctively, even though he gave no sign of it.

Surely someone looking so fit could not be sick. Could he be a doctor?

Intrigued, I dropped my case and raced the few yards to where the track veered sharply, curious to see if he would turn in at the big white building.

He flashed straight past, toward the dark copse and the Villa Caterina. He could be going no farther, for the track petered out there.

The truth hit me in a flash. He was none other than Enrico Gorini, the man I had journeyed across Europe to meet. The man who had met, married, and buried my dear Margaret in so short a space.

Chapter Four

The Via Santa Rosa proved to be the main street of Almina, so even though it was small and obscure, I found the Pensione Antonio without much trouble. And glad I was to reach its shelter, for the ill-paved road was crowded with rough and noisy citizens, who stared at me with frank and rude curiosity.

Dr. Crossley's description of passable did the place more than justice. It was downright seedy, if the dingy reception hall was anything to go by.

I walked to the untidy desk, behind which sat a plump woman in black and asked for a single room.

She stared curiously at me, perhaps because I looked so Italian yet spoke in English, then answered haltingly in the same tongue.

"For how long you wish to stay signorina?"

"I'm not sure. Not very long. You have a room for a short time?"

"*Si*, but you must pay in advance."

I paid the modest sum asked then signed the register she thrust before me.

"Lisa Moravia?" She sounded decidedly suspicious. "That is Italian. You look Italian yet speak English."

"I am Italian born!" I said impatiently. "Does the language matter so much?"

Shrugging her broad shoulders she handed me a key, at the same time bawling for Luigi.

There was no lift. The porter carried up my case, opened the shutters to let in some light, and left me.

Quite the largest cockroach I had ever seen scuttled across

the threadbare carpet. I gave a smothered scream and shook out the bedcover to make sure there were no more lurking about.

This was worse than anything I had ever experienced. My stay here would be as brief as possible, I determined. No wonder foreign visitors were few if this was the best accommodation available.

As it was already warm, I changed into a cotton frock and sandals, then thankfully left the dreary room and found a *carrozza* in the street. For now that I knew for certain Gorini was back, I should not again be put off seeing him.

Driving up the hill was pleasant enough with the slight breeze created and the countryside not yet browned off by the sun, but I felt distinctly queasy at the thought of storming the villa again after my reception of yesterday. How would the master react to me, and the woman I had glimpsed beside him? Who was she, I wondered.

Presently we were there. I paid off the driver and silently turned in at the gates. The tall cypress trees bordering the short drive closed in like brooding wraiths, shutting out the world beyond. I moved quietly to the front door, terrified of rousing that vicious dog again.

The blank eyes of the statues stared at me as I rang the bell and waited, but now the shutters of the lower windows were half raised, giving a slightly more lived-in appearance. And this time I did not have to ring a second time. The same unprepossessing individual opened the door and peered out at me.

"You again!" he growled.

"Of course. I told you I should be back. And don't pretend your master is still away. I saw him myself driving up this way a short time ago."

"That does not mean you will be welcome," he parried. "My master is in the garden with a visitor. Go round and find him if you must. I am much too busy to leave the house."

"What about that savage dog?" I asked angrily.

"Shut up today." With that the door was closed in my face. Fuming, I followed the neglected drive he had vaguely indicated that skirted the villa to the back. Here, facing south, I found myself in a different world from the shut-in oppressiveness of the front. Artistically laid out gardens, with fountains, statues, and low-clipped hedges sloped gently down toward extensive plantations. The source of the villa's wealth.

Beyond a riot of roses that smelled divine I heard voices. A woman's laugh as tinkling as a fountain, and a man's deeper voice. Suddenly diffident, I hesitated, but this was my last chance. If I funked it, I should never again dare to face that surly manservant.

Drawing a deep breath, I forced myself to go on.

The rose garden was a picture, highlighted by the fountain in the center that threw its sparkling jet high into the air, to fall back in rainbow cascades among the fat dolphins in the marble basins. And lounging on the bench beside it were a pair worthy of this luscious setting.

She had blue-black hair, warm olive skin, a scarlet mouth, and a figure superb in its rich dress. He, his arm about her, was as handsome in his equally Italian style as any man I had seen.

And I had certainly seen him before. On my long train journey, and again in the car that flashed past me.

They looked at me together, she with frank annoyance at this invasion of their privacy, he with a blank stare that changed to surprised recognition.

"The little signorina of the express," he said rising. "What odd chance brings you out here?"

"Didn't your manservant mention my calling yesterday? I had a most unpleasant reception."

At this the Italian beauty exploded. "*Dio, mio,* Enrico! Can we not even have privacy out in this wilderness now! Who is this girl who follows you around? Tell her to go away."

My eyes flashed as angrily as hers. "Since I was born in the Villa Caterina, I have as much right as you to be here! I came to see for myself the place that claimed both my mother's and my stepsister's lives."

Their expressions changed. He recovered first and said

smoothly, "So you are Lisa Moravia! Why did you give yourself all the trouble? I told you in my letter there was nothing for you here. Not even the ghost of poor Margaret, for she never really fitted in here. She loved only me."

"And you her inheritance, obviously," I stormed on, rashly, "or you would not have recovered so quickly from her tragic end." I glared at his companion.

He actually laughed. "How young and unsubtle you are, little Lisa. I forgive you, because of it. Carlotta Mancini and I are old friends. She is an opera singer. I adore her voice, and she adores me, as all women do. Can I help that?"

"Of all the conceited . . ." I broke off, realizing that anger would achieve nothing. "All I want," I finished flatly, "is a few of Margaret's possessions, then I shall be heartily glad to shake the dust of Calabria from my feet. The most barbarous region I ever encountered."

He frowned. "They are all locked away in her room. Naturally I have not cared to disturb them so soon. But maybe this afternoon? Perhaps you would care to stay to lunch?"

Carlotta Mancini exploded into a torrent of angry Italian, the gist of which obviously was that she did not in the least endorse his invitation.

"Don't worry," I said. "I shan't force myself where I'm not welcome."

He came and stood close, his hand on my shoulder.

"Today is difficult," he said, "but tomorrow Carlotta returns to Naples where she is singing at San Carlo. If you will come tomorrow for lunch, I shall keep the afternoon free for you. What do you say to that?"

I nodded. What else could I do. He was not the kind of man one could flout.

"Where are you staying? At the Pensione Antonio, I suppose?"

Again I inclined my head.

He grimaced. "The food is fit only for peasants. You must take a picnic lunch and eat it in the hills. It is too hot and dusty in the town."

He snapped his fingers at a passing gardener and issued instructions in Italian. The next moment I found myself following this individual to a kitchen at the back of the house.

The kitchen was huge, stone-flagged and ancient. It reeked of hot olive oil, garlic, and spices. At the cluttered bench stood a mountainous woman making pizza.

The gardener spoke to her in Italian and hastened back to his work. She smiled broadly at me and indicated with her floury hand a rush-bottomed chair.

"You want a picnic, *si?* No trouble, signorina. Do you like salami?"

"Not much."

"Then cheese and eggs it will be. I have plenty of both."

She slit open half a dozen rolls, plastered them with butter, added a wedge of cheese and a couple of hard-boiled eggs. This she placed in a straw bag with some ripe apricots and a half bottle of pale wine.

"Fit for the Pope," she beamed, handing it across.

I smiled in return.

"How kind you are. I'll return your bag tomorrow when I come to lunch."

"I make you something nice. *Arrivederci, signorina.*"

How different she was from the dour doorkeeper, I thought as I left the house and made for the gate.

Once outside my spirits rose. A picnic up here would be heaven. I pushed aside the nagging doubts about Margaret's death that had returned when I saw how lightly Enrico Gorini was taking it. Tomorrow I would face it again.

Today I would relax. Heaven knew I needed to after my recent tribulations. And what better way to start than by climbing up to the castle and seeing at close quarters if it would make an effective picture to sketch before I left this place forever.

By this time, even up here, it was very warm. Small green lizards basked on the stony, sun-baked track, darting away as I approached. Below sprawled the town, a huddle of flat red roofs and white walls, and a plume of smoke from a steam train in the station. Above, the somber castle grew larger as I drew near.

At first it seemed deserted. I passed through a rusting iron gate standing open, then through the gaping void where a door had once been, into the castle itself. Here I had to tread warily. Piles of broken masonry and stones lay around in the vast chamber. The window slits were crumbling into wider openings and in one corner the ceiling was down.

Outside it had been hot. Here a strange chill lay dankly. Broken steps led down to what must be dungeons below, while another set of stone steps led upward.

At close quarters the place was repellant, with no sketching possibilities, but from above there should be a wonderful view of the town below and the surrounding countryside. I might as well enjoy it, now that I had made the effort to get up here.

Halfway up the flight, a slight sound from below alerted me. I spun round to see an old man standing staring up at me.

He was roughly dressed and with the sallow skin of Calabria. He spoke no word nor expressed any welcome in his face, but simply stood with his baleful gaze.

A tiny tremor of fear went through me. He must have come up from the dungeons or in from another apartment. Was he the keeper of the castle? Surely such a ruin would need none.

In a small voice, I asked in English if there were any fee to be paid. He neither answered nor moved.

But when I turned to continue my upward climb, I knew instinctively that he was silently following me.

Panic threatened then, but as there was no room to pass him on the narrow open steps, I had no option but to go on.

I emerged onto a roof terrace, hemmed in by a broken balustrade. The view was indeed magnificent. How I should have enjoyed, had I been alone, to look my fill from every angle. But how could I ignore that silent presence standing by the descent, just watching and waiting for me to go?

It was an effort to force myself to walk past him at length and down the crazy steps, without rushing headlong and putting myself in danger. A swift glance back showed that he was silently following. I sped as swiftly as the rubble allowed through the ground floor chamber, out into the open air and through the rusted gates.

My heart was hammering in fear, my breath coming in gasps. A safe distance away I paused to calm down, and glanced back.

The old man had followed me to the gate. This he proceeded to clang shut, then fastened it with chain and padlock and turned a key.

The brief strange incident left a chill. That dour, unnerving silence of his had been more frightening than any angry outburst or demand for money. What a strange inhospitable region this was. How could Margaret have wanted to stay, and my mother before her. But now that I realized Enrico Gorini was none other than the stranger of the journey, and had met him again, I, too, had felt his force and magnetism, and knew that he was correct when he declared that Margaret had loved him rather than his environment. No doubt it had been the same with my mother and Pietro Moravia.

Now well away from the castle, I wandered along a faint track leading deeper into the hills, to find a congenial spot for my picnic. Presently I found it, a bank of coarse grass shaded by yellow broom, with only the darting lizards for company, and a buzzard wheeling silently overhead.

The fresh mountain air had made me hungry. I ate with relish, leaving only a roll and a little of the wine.

How pleasant it was up here. The hot, dusty town below had no such charm. Since time did not matter today, there was no point in hurrying back. I could explore further.

I followed the track until it became stony and hard on my sandaled feet, when a more inviting vista opened on my right. A luscious ravine, clothed with trees and greenery and flowering golden broom, with a ribbon of water flowing through it, fell sharply down, to rise even more steeply on the far side.

That must be the river that emerged in the town by the railway, I reasoned. If I climbed down and followed it, I should have a cool and pleasant walk back.

With bushes and rocks to give hand and foot holds, the descent should not be too difficult for one used to the wild Welsh mountain sides. With a light heart I began my careful climb down.

Halfway I met a rougher patch. Great boulders and rocks sprang up. Greater caution would be needed here. I sat down to rest for a few minutes, my back warm against a convenient stone.

The silence was profound. Drowsy in the sun that beat on this treeless stretch, I closed my eyes and almost drifted off to sleep.

Something roused me just before I lost consciousness. Some muffled but repeated sound that stole insistently into my mind, sounding a warning.

My eyes flew open. I listened intently. It was the sound of someone groaning. Somewhere, quite near, a fellow human was in pain.

My recent experiences here had done nothing to endear the natives to me or make me want to extend contact. But this was different. A sort of mayday signal. If someone had lost his footing in this wilderness, perhaps slipped and broken a bone, I might be the only one to come within earshot for days. Unless I went to his assistance, he could lie there until he perished.

There was no shirking responsibility.

Quietly I rose and began to pick my way toward the sound, moving among much more towering rocks now. Whoever it was, was well hidden. I could see no trace of a living soul. Then, as I peered about in mystification, I heard something that froze me in my tracks.

Another voice, richly Italian, spoke soothingly as though to comfort the one in trouble.

So the sufferer was not alone. My help would not be needed. Now all I wanted was to get away without being seen, since Dr. Crossley's warning of a strange and sinister aura hanging over the place came flooding back to me. A stronghold of the Mafia he had said. Had I stumbled on a hideout of theirs?

Hastily I turned to retreat, but my quick movement dislodged a stone that clattered down the slope with staccato intensity.

Instantly, there was a loud oath, and from behind a bush of golden broom, hanging from a crevice in a rock, a man thrust himself out. Ragged, dirty, and ugly, he was well calculated to quell the stoutest heart. He certainly quelled mine as with a few agile leaps he reached and grabbed hold of me.

I shook my head at his torrent of words, murmuring, "English."

Surprisingly he answered in the same language, with a harsh "What do you want here?"

"Nothing particularly. I was merely climbing down to the river when I heard a groan. I figured someone was in need of help."

His black eyes took in my Italian coloring. Skepticism showed on his face and grasping my arm, he dragged me back to the bush, through its curtaining trailers and into a cave.

I blinked until my eyes adjusted themselves to the dimmer light. My captor was talking rapidly in Italian. A moment or two and then I saw the man to whom his words were addressed.

He lay on a bed of dried grass. Almost as unkempt as the one who grasped me, he still had an air of distinction about him. And here was the groaner, without doubt. A blood-stained rag was wound around his head, another round his shin from which his trouser leg had been rolled.

"You are hurt!" I exclaimed in quick sympathy. "Is there anything I can do to help?"

His velvety-brown eyes stared up at me. "Why do you speak in English when you are obviously Italian?"

Once again I had to explain that I had spent my entire life in Britain. "But enough of me. You look as though you need skilled help badly," I ended, troubled by the pallor showing through his bronzed skin, and the weary set of his mouth. "Surely I can help?"

He eyed the bag I clutched with desperate hope.

"Only if you happen to have something eatable about you. *Dio, mio,* I'm ravenous!"

I dropped to my knees beside him, produced the wine bottle and uncorked it. He snatched it with desperate eagerness and drained the small quantity in a few gulps. The buttered roll went the same way in seconds. He seemed almost starving.

"I do wish I had more." I glanced unhappily from him to his rough companion, standing guard over me. "The town of Almina is not far off," I added. "You could get food there, and help too. I'm willing to stay with your sick friend, if you don't like to leave him."

"No!" my captor exploded.

I looked again at the man on the ground. "So you don't trust me? If you have something to hide, I assure you I can be very discreet."

"You don't in the least understand," the wounded man declared. "For reasons of our own, Angelo does not care to be seen in daylight."

"You are members of the Mafia perhaps?" I declared, greatly daring.

He laughed shortly. "Think what you please." His pain-wracked eyes glared at me as though they would read my very soul.

His companion spoke warningly in Italian, too rapid for me to follow.

"You'll have to trust me you know," I said in a matter-of-fact way. "Otherwise it's a safe bet that either starvation or your wounds will end your troubles pretty quickly. If Angelo dare not show his face abroad, I'll go and bring food back myself and anything else you need."

"I can go myself under cover of darkness," Angelo growled.

"Your friend doesn't look as if he could wait that long. He really ought to have skilled help you know. The Almina hospital isn't very far. Dr. Crossley's awfully kind. I'm sure he'd admit him and give him any treatment necessary."

"You know the hospital?" the sick man said quickly. "Say, who are you? A nurse?"

I shook my head. "Simply a visitor from Britain who happened to be bitten by a dog." I showed him my wrist. "They were very kind to me."

The two men conferred in Italian. At last Carlo, as the patient was evidently named, looked at me.

"You are here for a brief visit only then returning to your own country. You swear to that?"

I shrugged. "What have I to gain by lies?"

"Then we must trust you, but first swear you'll keep your mouth shut about what you've seen here. Forget everything as soon as the episode is closed."

Hand on heart I solemnly agreed. What else could I do?

He struggled into a sitting position, turning even paler as his head swam. Angelo placed a bulging rucksack behind him to give some support, and Carlo looked at me.

"I suppose it is too much to expect you to produce paper and pencil from that bag of yours?"

"Not at all. I always carry a notebook when abroad. It comes in useful for jotting down new words as I learn them." I passed it to him and watched as he began to write.

He tore out the page, folded it, and handed it to me with the pencil and notebook.

"Go straight to the hospital," he instructed, "but not to the front entrance. Around at the back you will find a small building labeled 'Dispensary.' Knock three times. If a gray-haired man with a beard opens it, give the password."

"Which is?"

"Swordfish calling. Repeat it please."

"Swordfish calling," I repeated obediently.

"Don't forget it and don't ever mention it to another soul. If the old dispenser isn't alone, make some excuse and call back later."

"And after I've given the password and your written message?"

"He'll give you bandages and other medicaments. Are you well enough disposed to bring them here to me in absolute secrecy?"

His velvet-brown eyes challenged me. There was something in them, and the proud lift of his battered countenance, that pulled at my heart strings.

"Of course, but you ought to be in hospital."

"I know that. This confounded bullet will have to be removed before I'm good for anything."

"Bullet!" I said with concern. "Where?"

"In the calf of my leg. Don't worry, I'll survive. The old dispenser will send help after dark. Now go with all speed and if you can lay hands on anything eatable, fetch that too, for the love of heaven! Above all, talk to no one except the dispenser."

I picked up my rush bag and thrust my way out through the bushy curtain. The glance Angelo threw my way proved that he at least only half-trusted me. He growled something to the effect that if I betrayed them I should not live to see Britain again.

Here was a strange kettle of fish into which I had landed myself I reflected as I began the climb back. The Mafia, if such they were, were a ruthless gang of extortionists and murderers against whom Dr. Crossley had expressly warned me. Why oh why had I been drawn into their net?

What would have happened, I wondered, had I not volunteered help. Had they not grudgingly accepted it? Angelo would never have let me loose to betray them.

Shuddering, I pictured a quick flash of his knife and my body hurtling down to the river below.

But now there was nothing to stop me going straight to David Crossley, telling him the whole story, and letting him deal with it, while I kept well away from the hills and the ravine, if I were so inclined.

The thought was discarded as soon as it took shape. I had given my word. There was no going back on it. Besides, a pair of brown pain-filled eyes haunted me. Surely Carlo, at least, could be guilty of nothing really despicable. I would not believe that.

What was written on that scrap of paper? Would it throw any light on the mystery? Under the circumstances I had a moral right to know, I decided, as on reaching the top of the ravine, I extricated it from my notebook.

Not only was it written in Italian, but also in code, so was beyond my comprehension. Perhaps just as well for my peace of mind.

It was now the hottest part of the afternoon. Perspiration broke out as I hurried along the solitary, stony path through air that seemed to quiver in a heat haze.

The mysterious castle loomed up. I glanced fearfully at it as I passed, but the gates were still closed. With a rush I took the downward track, then turned right for the short walk to the hospital.

This at least looked sane and serene as I approached the trim white building and took the path that led round to the back.

There was the small building marked "Dispensary." I waited until a nurse, her arms full of supplies, had disappeared into the main building, then gave the three knocks on the door.

It was opened almost immediately by an elderly man whose description fitted the one given to me. He peered at me from behind his spectacles.

"Swordfish calling," I said boldly.

He drew me inside and closed the door.

As he was alone, I produced the note.

He read it, tut-tutted, and demanded to know how it had come into my possession. Briefly I told him.

Silently he took various things from his supply cupboards and thrust them into my bag.

A used luncheon tray stood on the table. The pasta dish was empty, but rolls, cheese, and a half bottle of wine were left.

"The sick man is ravenously hungry," I said on impulse. "If I could take what is left on the tray . . ."

"*Si, si!*" He wrapped the food in a paper napkin, thrust it and the wine in with the medical supplies, then urged me to the door, first glancing out to make sure that no one was in sight.

"*Avante.* Go quickly before anyone comes in, signorina. Tell the patient, some time tonight, and above all, be cautious."

"*Grazie, signore.*" Infinitely glad of this prospect of more practical help for the wounded man, I left the building, only to come face to face with Dr. Crossley, about to enter his car at the front door.

He looked surprised to see me. "Why, Miss Moravia, I trust your wrist is giving no trouble?"

"Oh, no, Doctor." I had to think furiously. Much as I longed to confide in this man, I did not know whether he was in liaison with the dispenser, so I must conceal the purpose for my presence at all costs. "It's simply that having time on my hands, I was walking up here and thought I'd take another glance at the hospital my father built," I added.

"By all means. Well now, if you're ready to go back to town, hop in. I'm on my way down there to see a patient, and it's not the time of day for pleasant walking."

"Oh, but I'm going into the hills," I said quickly. "I must see them at close quarters before I leave the district. I sketch, you know."

"As you please, but don't wander too far alone." He seemed about to say more, then changed his mind and stepped into his car.

"*Arrivederci,*" he called as he pulled away.

Brows drawn, I hurried back the way I had come, wishing one moment that I could see beneath the surface of this strange situation, and the next moment glad that I should soon be shaking the dust of it from my shoes. Secrecy and subversion seemed to be everywhere, and already, against my will, I had been drawn into it. How providential that I should soon be safely back in Wales.

I was perspiring freely when I reached the spot where I made the descent into the ravine. I climbed down, found the trailing broom bush that so effectively concealed the entrance to the cave, parted it, and entered.

How silent everything was. For a moment I fancied the two men had vanished and the cave was empty. Then my eyes adjusting, I saw Carlo lying there alone, his eyes closed.

I knelt down beside him. How wan he looked and how defenseless. Again I felt the warm stirring of my heart strings as my gaze lingered on the tumbled black hair above the soiled bandage, the sensitive curve of his lip, the dark lashes resting on his cheeks.

Perhaps my intensity registered. The dark lashes were raised. Eyes brown and velvety looked up at me.

"So you're back, signorina. Bravo."

"My name's Lisa," I said. "Everything went without a hitch. I have medical supplies and a snack. Where's Angelo?"

"Gone down to the river for water. He talked of trying to catch a fish. He's had nothing to eat since yesterday, poor fellow."

"Then we'd better save him half the rolls." I fished them out. There were four. Two of them I put aside. The others and the cheese I gave to Carlo after propping him up with the rucksack.

He ate, and drank the wine with appreciation.

"You're an angel, Lisa," he said as he set down the bottle. "It was a miracle, your chancing to come this way. Normally this ravine is deserted. That is why it makes such a good hideout."

"I shan't ask any questions," I said slowly. "Whatever you and Angelo are up to, that's your business. However, I *would* like to know where you learned such very good English. Surely not in this wilderness."

"Of course not. I'm a Neapolitan by birth. My father was a wealthy merchant and sent me to the finest schools. Since he was also an ardent Royalist he clashed violently with the Fascist regime that grew up. He was killed and his estates confiscated. So I joined a band who work against them secretly. As you've doubtless guessed, we're all wanted outlaws, working underground. Those caught are either murdered or sent to the *confino* for life imprisonment. Now you understand the desperate need for secrecy."

I nodded. "I suppose the dispenser is one of your contacts, working with you. Oh, while I remember, he said to tell you, 'Some time tonight.' That means you'll be taken into proper care, I hope. But right now I'd better change those bandages for you as there's no one else to do it."

I was a complete novice in the art of nursing, but I unwound the grubby head bandage with no visible show of revulsion, even when congealed blood on the forehead was laid bare.

"That's nothing to worry about," he said. "Just put on some antiseptic and a clean bandage. It's the bullet in the leg that worries me."

With no water available, there was nothing else I could do. I finished that then did the same for his leg, where a bullet was lodged in the calf. How long ago was it that he had been shot at? I wondered.

"With luck, they'll operate and have it out before morning," he said as I finished. "A handful of the staff are in league with us, secretly of course. We couldn't work effectively without such loyal contacts to aid and abet us."

"I wonder if Dr. Crossley is among them," I murmured. "He's English and I'm sure would always back right against might, yet he warned me about the presence of—" I broke off, reluctant to use the term Mafia again, since these two had not admitted to it.

He shrugged. "Names are used as little as possible. The dispenser is our first contact. Why Angelo! Caught any fish?"

I spun round as he entered noiselessly. The momentary glimpse of the outside showed a darkening of the sky. Dusk would soon be here.

"I must go!" I said in a panic. "I don't fancy losing myself in this wilderness in the dark. Good luck to you both, and pray all goes well with your leg, Carlo."

He clasped the hand I held out to him, warmly and firmly.

Strangely, I hated the thought of saying good-bye.

"Shall I ever see you again, I wonder," I said impulsively.

"Who knows. What has to be, will be. But in your small way you have helped our cause. *Arrivederci*, and many thanks."

With that I was forced to leave him, knowing that whatever happened, I left a small corner of my heart in that desolate cave, deep in the wilderness of Calabria.

Were they members of the Mafia, or not? If so, surely all members were not the villains David Crossley had implied. Did that kindly man know what was going on in his own hospital beneath his very nose?

It was all most confusing. Shaking my head in perplexity, I hastened on my way back to the seedy pensione.

Chapter Five

I finished my chunk of bread and cherry jam at breakfast next morning and left the stale-smelling dining room with relief. Yet the prospect ahead, of my luncheon engagement at the Villa Caterina, curiously held no attraction. Was it the thought of seeing dear Margaret's possessions and the room in which she had died? Or the prospect of meeting Enrico Gorini? Or the knowledge that tomorrow I should be making reservations for my journey back to Wales? Surely that fact should have brought satisfaction, yet oddly it did not.

The sun was not yet fierce enough to make the uphill walk a burden, so I arrived at the villa feeling fresh and cool in my flowered cotton dress. Enrico was pacing about outside the front door, looking decidedly impatient.

"So! *Buona giorno, signorina.* I have to pay my morning visit to the citrus groves. Will you walk there with me or wait inside?"

"Oh, the citrus groves certainly." I had never seen one at close quarters, and soon I should be far away from such exotic trees. "Are they oranges or lemons, or both?"

"Both, but chiefly bergamots," he said as we moved off together round to the back of the house and through the gardens.

"Bergamots? Now there's something I've never heard of."

He laughed, displaying flashing white teeth. With head thrown back and eyes dancing he was extraordinarily attractive. I could see clearly how Margaret had fallen for him. Yet somehow the attraction was that of a sleek tiger or a black panther, rather than a handsome male.

"It's fortunate for us here in Italy that you and most of the world besides have *not* heard of them. This particular species, monorda, grows only in Calabria."

"But what is so rare about just another type of lemon or orange?" I demanded.

"The fact, little Lisa, that the fragrant oil, when extracted from the fruit, is an essential ingredient of some of the finest perfume in the world. Most of our supply is sold to the Parisian houses. As a matter of fact, I was returning from a business trip connected with that when I encountered you on the train."

A business trip when he had only just buried his bride of a few weeks, I thought with fierce anger. Proof enough what his feeling for her had been.

I fought down the anger as, the gardens behind us, we paused on ground sloping gently to the south. Before us lay acres and acres of neat rows of small trees, from which a heady perfume stole out. Orange blossom, lemon tang, and something different from either.

Narrow conduits of water intersected the groves, and from these girondales flung rainbow spray high into the air, passing life-giving moisture to the trees.

Moving nearer, I saw that blossom, immature fruit, and ripe golden balls sprouted simultaneously, something I had never seen on any tree back home.

"We have our own extraction plant for the bergamots," Enrico explained. "A thriving business and a lucrative one."

No wonder he had coveted it, I reflected somberly. What incredible fortune for him that Margaret had fallen so hopelessly under his spell, then succumbed to that deadly disease. But was it fate, or something more sinister that had cut her down?

On impulse I took from my pocket the strange note Margaret had sent me and passed it to him. I had read it so often that now I knew it off by heart. Swiftly the disturbing words passed through my mind.

Good-bye, darling Lisa. I just had to say it while I can still hold a pen. I know I shall never see you again, and the happy times we planned together out here can never be. It is too late for regrets now. Make your home permanently at our beloved Nantallon, which I leave to you, and forget Italy if you value your happiness. There seems to be a curse on the villa.

Your loving Margaret

"You may as well know it was this note that decided me to come out here," I said, "even before I received the news of Margaret's death. I feel I'm entitled to an explanation."

He actually shrugged. "So! For the love of heaven, don't let a sick woman's fancies worry you, Lisa. Had I known the contents, I'd never have let her send that note."

"A sick woman? Why, she was an exceptionally healthy person!"

"True. All that ailed her at the time was a little digestive upset due to the unaccustomed rich food and wine of the country. But as the cholera outbreak was just beginning here, she was convinced she had caught it, and panicked. It wasn't the case. Unfortunately, later on, she really did catch the bug with fatal results."

It sounded plausible, but somehow I was not convinced. Not where practical and sensible Margaret was concerned.

"May I have that note please?"

He slipped it into his pocket. "No. I won't have you worrying over an illusion. There are too many genuine worries in this world."

Two angry spots of color flared in my cheeks.

"You may be master here now, signore, but you have no authority over me!"

Now he actually laughed. "What a storm over nothing! Come and see the building where the presses are. Most interesting, I assure you."

There was no withstanding him. Suddenly I hated this man. All I wanted now was to collect a few of Margaret's personal things and leave the place forever.

I took only a cursory interest in the rest of the walk round and was glad when we were back in the villa.

After a glass of Marsala from Sicily, I followed him up the marble staircase to a small room, cool as a morgue and darkened by closed shutters. These he opened. A flood of sunlight disclosed the sparse furnishings and plain single bed.

I must have shown my surprise for he said, "Of course this was not her own bedroom. Simply where we isolated her when she caught the wretched cholera."

There on the rickety-looking dressing table were her things. Tears sprang to my eyes as they rested on her tortoiseshell brush and comb, her gold wristwatch, and a small bottle of her favorite cologne.

He grasped my hand. "Painful, is it not? Better to try and forget."

I tore away my hand. "I'll take the hairbrush and the watch," I said in a choked voice, prepared to do battle if he objected.

He merely nodded. "Of course. Anything you wish. I have no use for them."

At that moment the ugly retainer, whose name it transpired was Guido Spadoni, knocked and entered to say that Enrico was wanted on the phone.

"Take your time," Enrico said as he moved to the door. "I'll see you downstairs. Lunch will soon be ready."

With set face I placed the few things in the capacious handbag I had brought with me, then stood looking at the bed, trying to visualize Margaret lying there. If only I could have seen her before she died. If only she could have poured out her secret fears to me, I should have had a weapon at my disposal. Now, with even her note confiscated, I had nothing. All I could do was return to Wales and forget this ill-fated villa as she had warned me.

As in a dream I descended the marble staircase into the mosaic-floored hall. Through an open doorway from a room that looked like a study came Enrico's voice, still at the phone.

I passed inside. The room was lofty and opulent looking, lined on two sides with bookcases, on the other with rich tapestry. A leather-topped desk, at which sat Enrico, dominated the room. The papers on it were neat and tidy. My glance fell on a standing calendar as I waited. The date shown was June 10, 1940.

Enrico put down the instrument and rose, an air of great excitement about him.

"I'm ready to go now," I said flatly. "I see no point in staying for lunch. I have to make arrangements to return home as soon as possible."

"Oh no," he said. "You won't be returning home yet."

"Whatever can you mean?"

"Mussolini has joined forces with Hitler and declared war on France and England. We are, my dear Lisa, now enemies of your adopted country."

I stared in stupefaction. "But I *have* to get back! I can't stay here. The place is hateful to me."

He shrugged. "Reflect, dear girl. You were born in this very house, so you are indisputably Italian. As such you are safe enough here. But try to travel out to enemy country and you'll come up against formidable difficulties. In fact, you'd run the risk of arrest and detention as a spy, with your mixed background. No. I'm afraid, whether you like it or not, you are here for the duration of hostilities."

A terrible sense of being trapped closed in on me.

"Don't look so scared," he said, walking round the desk and placing his hand on my shoulder. "I realize your resources out here are negligible and you are in a precarious position. Forget it. After all, this is—or was—your home. Look on it that way while you are forced to remain in Calabria. Heaven 'nows the place is big enough. No need to get on each other's nerves."

His hand bit into my shoulder, his eyes burned into mine. Absurd as it was, it seemed that he had planned it all to trap me under this roof. With limited money, and even the tawdry Pensione Antonio soon beyond my means, I should eventually be driven to accepting his hateful hospitality.

"Not unless I'm forced to," I said somberly, "I'd rather stay at the Pensione Antonio."

He laughed sardonically. "Until you find a cockroach in your soup, I venture to think. Then you'll be glad to avail yourself of something better. Oh well, so be it. Come and go as you please, if only for a meal. I promise not to say 'I told you so.'"

I scarcely heard. The single advantage to come out of this disaster of war was that I could still remain in contact with that dear Dr. Crossley. And even the enigmatic Carlo would not be too far off, though we were destined never to meet again, it seemed.

Such an impact had these two men made on my susceptible young heart, that the thought was like a silver lining to a dark cloud.

Chapter Six

I should die of boredom, imprisoned in this backwater for an indefinite period, I reflected the following morning, as I drank my second cup of luke-warm coffee, while a slatternly waiter set out cutlery on the adjoining table. True, my first days had been anything but boring, but the initial shocks were over now. What else could possibly happen here?

Plump Signora Petulengro now came bustling in, her black eyes snapping with excitement.

"Have you heard the news, signorina?" she twittered. "We are now at war with France and Britain. You had better keep quiet about your British connections if you wish to keep out of trouble!"

"I'm not ashamed of them," I said coldly. "My main regret is that the trouble will prevent my returning there at once. I can't wait to leave Almina behind."

"Is that so! Well, you may have to leave this pensione quicker than you thought. This morning I have word of a party of nuns and children being evacuated here from a small convent in Napoli. It will be safer for the children, and the hill air good for them. Sister Theresa's family live in Almina, so she immediately thought of my refuge. I do not think we shall have any vacant rooms then, signorina."

She bustled away drawing the waiter with her and scolding that he would have to work harder when the new arrivals eventually turned up.

I grimaced. The press of events seemed to be forcing me toward the Villa Caterina, whether I willed it or not.

Meanwhile, I had the day to fill, and in my keyed-up state,

sketching or painting was impossible. Activity was essential, and where else but the road leading up into the hills.

So gladly I left the frowsty room and made my way over the broken pavements whereon shopkeepers were setting out their wares and shrill-voiced customers beginning to collect.

From a little Franciscan church two white-robed nuns stepped, still telling their beads and murmuring their Hail Mary's. The sun glinted like fire on the gold crosses hanging at their waists as they passed me, heads bowed.

A wayside shrine, decked with drooping flowers ended Almina.

The peace of the road winding up into the hills was profound and welcome, as though evil could never encroach. Yet behind the scenes it lurked in several guises, I knew.

At the top, where it curved for the hospital and the villa, I paused to catch my breath, staring up at the ruined castle, less austere in morning sunshine.

A car stood by the outer gate, sleek and shining, and as I speculated, a man emerged from the gateway, jumped into the vehicle and came purring down the hill.

Enrico Gorini, I realized in surprise.

He reached the crossroad and stopped abruptly when he saw me.

"So!" he exclaimed. "Already you have had enough of the Pensione Antonio and seek more comfort. Go ahead. I have some business to attend to in town but shall be back for lunch."

I shook my head.

"I'm simply taking a stroll. Mornings are lovely in the hills before it grows too hot. Why, even the old castle looks mellow this morning, though I shan't venture in there again."

"Again? Go on."

"Oh, I went inside the first day, but it was quite creepy with a strange old man following me around. Surely such a ruin doesn't have a keeper?"

"Keep away from the place," he said harshly. "The locals do."

"Yet you've just been there."

"I'm not a young and vulnerable stranger. Ruthless characters

drift up there at times, with scant regard for anyone. Stay away
for your own good."

I bit my lip. "I certainly shall, but that won't bar me from
wandering in the hills. I must pass the time somehow in this
backwater."

"The outbreak of war has certainly come at an inconvenient
time for you," he agreed. "Well, make for the villa after your
walk, and take lunch. It will be a cut above the pensione's
menu, I can promise you."

"Perhaps I'll be forced to take advantage of the villa and your
offer soon," I called as he drove off, recalling the advent of the
convent school and the signora's threat about my room. Could
he be connected with some secret organization, I wondered. On
the same side as Carlo, or not?

A bird of prey wheeling silently over the wooded ravine in
the hills recalled my adventure of yesterday. How *was* Carlo?
I wondered. Had the bullet been removed yet?

With the hospital so close, surely it would do no harm to
call and find out. Not if I were careful.

So I set off briskly toward it, my heart beating a little faster
at the thought of him. Though unlikely that I should ever see
him again, I could not put him out of my mind.

Someone who looked like a doctor was entering the dispensary as I stole into the back patio. I hung about out of sight
until he left with supplies, then hurried to the door and
knocked three times.

The old dispenser opened it. I gave the password. He drew
me inside and closed the door.

"You are the signorina who brought a message yesterday, are
you not?" he said. "You should not have come again. It is too
risky."

Crestfallen, I murmured, "I only wanted to know if the bullet
had been removed and if Carlo will recover."

He nodded. "He was operated on during the night, so should
eventually be all right. He probably owes his life to you, for
the bullet was removed just in time to prevent fatal consequences, I believe. For that I must thank you. You are brave

and kind, but now you must forget the incident completely for your own sake and ours, signorina."

Thoroughly deflated now I turned to go, but the door opened and in walked David Crossley.

He stopped dead when he saw me, staring first at me and then at the dispenser. Was he in the secret league or not?

Evidently, for the older man gave a short explanation in Italian, after which the doctor faced me with a brief smile.

"Bravo, signorina. I had no idea you were instrumental in getting the casualty to hospital. At the same time I deplore your becoming involved with danger. It is bad, bad."

He paused, frowning, then continued. "We must not stay here talking. At any moment nurses, orderlies may come in. The staff is not in our secret organization. They will wonder at your presence, perhaps gossip. Come with me."

He hastily wound a length of bandage over the small dressing on my wrist.

"Now hold it up conspicuously as though you were in pain," he instructed. "It will look as though you were being treated."

I followed him out. We met no one until we reached the waiting room, crowded with patients. He hurried me through this and into his private office, where he carefully closed the door and the wide-open window.

"You must be rapidly reaching the conclusion that we're all mad in Calabria," he said, motioning me to sit down. "What with your reception at the Villa Caterina and now this startling incident. I warned you that the region was a strange place with violent undertones. I'm only sorry that you had to come up against them in your brief visit. When are you leaving, by the way?"

"I'm not, unfortunately. Has the news of the outbreak of war with Britain not reached you, Doctor? Technically, I'm now an enemy of that country and must remain here for the duration whether I like it or not."

He looked grave. "I'd forgotten your complicated circumstances. How very unfortunate for you."

I nodded. "The worst prospect will be filling my time. I can visualize myself going slowly mad from sheer boredom. If only I could be of use somewhere, I shouldn't mind so much, but what prospect of that is there here, knowing no one?"

He did not answer immediately. He seemed to be debating with himself whether to speak out or not. At last he said hesitantly, "I don't suppose you've had any experience of nursing, by any chance?"

"Not experience, but I did take a course in first aid last summer. You see, my half sister ran a children's riding school in which I helped when at home. Falls were frequent out in the rough hill country, so that the person in charge needed to be capable of bandaging and other measures."

"Indeed. I suppose the course covered temperature taking and that sort of thing?"

"Why yes." Comprehension brought an eager flush to my face. "Do you mean, Doctor, that you might possibly find a use for me in your hospital? If only you could!"

"Not in the main wards," he said decisively. "Almina provides as many helpers as we want for those. What I had in mind is quite different. Secret, confidential, and above all, hazardous. In short, work for exceptional and courageous individuals. You have so far shown signs of those qualities, I think."

"Thank you. Do go on."

"We have a highly secret underground ward, for cases such as you helped yesterday, signorina. I should never have dreamed of mentioning it had not fate already involved you, and had you not been desperate for something to do. I, in turn, am desperate at times for helpers I can trust implicitly. My devoted charge nurse is seriously overworked, but carries on somehow. Three hours' help most mornings would greatly ease her burdens. Bed making and such, leaving her more time for the highly skilled work. I wonder if it would be asking too much of you. The secrecy and danger I mean?"

The thought of Carlo, suffering perhaps for want of attention, made me shake my head. "Is it connected with the Mafia?" I asked, hoping he would deny it, for the idea of Carlo and Angelo involved with such a gang was not at all palatable.

He only said, "If you are joining our organization, the first thing you must learn is never to ask questions. The less you know, the better for your safety and ours. All I can say is that it is nothing to be ashamed of. On the contrary, you would be helping the oppressed masses of Italy to a better life."

"A worthy enough cause, since I was born Italian," I said, "and I can't thank you enough for giving me the chance. When would you like me to start? Now?"

He smiled briefly at my eagerness.

"First swear that you will never reveal anything of what goes on here to a living soul other than fellow members."

Hand on heart, I solemnly swore, ending, "So help me God."

"Now I'll show you Swordfish Ward, as we call it," he said rising.

I rose with alacrity and impulsively grasped his hand.

"Oh, Dr. Crossley, how can I thank you for giving me an incentive while I'm forced to hang on here! I was really dreading it!"

How nice he was when a half-smile softened his mobile mouth. A classic English gentleman, with his fair hair and skin pale by comparison with the Calabrians. I could have kissed him had I not remembered that I was now no longer a child and must show restraint.

What he saw in my upturned face framed by its dark hair I could not know, but something in his expression made me blush and turn away.

"There's a hidden way down to Swordfish Ward behind the dispensary," he said. "We use it after dark to admit and discharge patients. I myself have my own secret way down there."

A second door in his office opened onto a long narrow passage that, in turn, led to a book-lined study.

"My private suite," he said, "with bedroom attached."

I stared in surprise. It was in complete contrast to the cool simplicity of the rest of the hospital, with its somber paneled walls, high painted ceiling, and narrow windows that let in little of the bright sunshine.

"This looks much older than the rest, Doctor."

"It is. Long ago this was a smaller villa on the estate—kept for the dowagers. When your father decided to build a hospital, he pulled it down to use the foundations. For some reason this wing was left standing. I annexed it for my own use when I took over as head."

I nodded. "A peaceful retreat from the stress of the hospital."

"Indeed. Better still there's a hidden entrance to the extensive cellars below. No doubt they were originally intended for wine and olive oil storage, but have now been converted to our secret purpose."

He opened the door of a cupboard wherein hung coats and suits. Stepping inside, he pressed a hidden spring high on the wall.

With a click, the back panel slid smoothly to one side disclosing a flight of stone steps that led steeply down.

"I suspect this was also used as a bolt hole in the bad old days of intrigue," he said, flashing on a torch and leading the way down. "I discovered it quite by accident soon after taking over."

Keyed up, I followed him down to a corridor that gave onto a cool chamber lighted only artificially. A dozen beds lined the walls, most occupied, but Carlo was not among them.

David Crossley spoke in Italian to a slim woman in white with serene face and a kindly smile, then introduced her as Nurse Ponti.

"Without her this place could not function," he said. "She and her assistant, Luigi, run the place between them. Your help will be a Godsend."

"Indeed," Nurse Ponti endorsed, "especially on the occasions when night work keeps us up, and we need to rest during the day, such as last night for instance."

"How *is* the new patient?" he asked, adding to me, "We have our own tiny theater down here, where Nurse Ponti and I perform necessary operations, with Luigi as anesthetist."

Such as removing the bullet from Carlo's calf, I reflected as I followed them into a smaller cell with only one bed in which he lay.

Clean and pale, a bandage like a halo round his brow, he sat propped up with pillows, looking angelic. A bed cradle over his injured leg made a bump in the bedclothes.

He grinned cheerfully at me, and the angelic illusion fled. "A thousand thanks, signorina. I believe I owe my life to you. A sly puss, I must say, not letting on that you were in the league."

"I've only just joined, since the outbreak of war makes it impossible for me to return to England now," I explained.

"War! *Dio, mio,* and I immobilized here. Our work will be even more vital now. For the love of heaven, get me moving again as fast as you can, Doctor."

"We'll throw you out as soon as possible, never fear. In the meantime just be patient and co-operative, especially when Signorina Lisa is in charge of you. She's inexperienced but thirsting to help out. Fitting, really, since her own father founded and his money still maintains the place, don't you think?"

Carlo stared, suspicion and hostility plainly visible.

"But I believed her British! You can't mean she's staying at the Villa Caterina with the villain Gorini, and has insinuated herself into our midst!" he growled.

"I'm at the Pensione Antonio, and I've no reason to love Gorini since he's contrived to rob me of the villa and estate!" I flared back.

"Enough of this!" Dr. Crossley snapped. "It was a trick of fate really that forced my hand, by Lisa discovering and helping you. I'm certain she means well and can be implicitly trusted. Now there let the matter end. You both know the rules. Silence is golden. And now I must get back to upstairs work before I'm missed."

He turned to me. "When you leave, use the same way as we came. We can pretend that you are working for me doing hospital clerical work a few hours a week. That way the staff won't be curious if they notice your comings and goings. The same excuse can be made to anyone else interested in your movements. And now I leave her to you, Nurse Ponti."

He hurried off. Nervously I glanced at the older woman.

"Bring the tray of dressings from my desk in the main ward," she said. "We'll go round together this morning, then tomorrow, you might manage some on your own. Luigi is sleeping at present. He does the bulk of the night duties."

All through her ministrations, I felt Carlo's brooding gaze fixed upon me. It made my efforts to help even more fumbling. He seemed just as uncertain and wary of me as I of him. If only I knew more of this organization in which I had become enmeshed. It was becoming clearer, however, that with a man like Dr. Crossley involved, the aims must be honorable. And Carlo? I was not so sure. Yet given the same circumstances, I should not hesitate to help him again, however dangerous it might make life for me.

As though he read my thoughts, his sensitive mouth creased into an almost reluctant smile as I bent to ease the pillow behind him.

Chapter Seven

I was through by twelve-thirty and left the hospital as unobtrusively as possible.

Though hectic, the morning had been interesting. I should certainly go again tomorrow on an honorary basis, so that I should feel under no obligation if circumstances altered.

Hungry as I was, lunch at the villa would have been welcome, but I did not want to face Gorini just yet. He would probably ask how I had filled my morning, and I had not yet had time to school myself in the evasion necessary. It would be like skating on thin ice, discussing my work at the hospital with his black eyes boring into me.

So I walked down to the Pensione Antonio and settled for minestrone soup and fruit at the table by the window, grubby cloth and all.

I was the only customer, yet kept waiting. The signora brought in the food herself at last and dumped it on the table with a gusty sigh.

"*Dio, mio*, what a morning! We are all run off our feet. The nuns and *bambini* arrive tomorrow, we hear by phone. Such short notice, and such a crowd! Four beds to a room we have to make up. You can stay tonight, but must go tomorrow, signorina."

"So soon!"

"It cannot be helped. You will easily find a room in a private house. They will be glad of the money."

Visualizing the dingy dwellings with no privacy or conveniences, I grimaced. The Villa Caterina, with all its sinister undertones, would be preferable.

"I'll take my case and go today," I told her, realizing that it would be difficult in the morning with my new job. Living at the villa, I would at least be nearer my work.

I rested until the worst of the afternoon heat had passed then hired a taxi and left Almina, glad now that Gorini had thrown out his invitation of hospitality. Entering the gates of the villa felt rather like entering the spider's web, but there was no help for it.

I had only just paid off the driver and was about to ring the bell when another car drove up, a much more opulent one, and out stepped Carlotta Mancini, also complete with case.

The stare she cast my way was distinctly hostile.

"Surely you, too, are not moving into the villa!" she demanded.

"Since I've been turned out of the pensione by the exigencies of war and Signor Gorini suggested it, I've no option," I declared.

"I, too, am a refugee from Napoli owing to the exigencies of war," she lamented. "The management of San Carlo have decided to close the theater until they see how things go. They fear a key port like Napoli may be heavily bombed by the British or French. I don't care to take the risk of lingering there myself, with such a splendid retreat in these hills."

How would Enrico Gorini react to this double invasion I wondered as we rang the bell.

If Spadoni was surprised to see us he scarcely showed it, merely informing us that the master was in his study if we cared to go in.

"The master is right here," boomed Gorini's voice as he made his appearance. "Now what is this? A deputation?"

Carlotta rushed toward him.

"Oh Enrico, the theater has closed and I was so scared of air raids, I had to get out. Are you not pleased to see me?" she gushed.

"I'm even more desperate," I added. "I've been turned out of the pensione to make way for a party of refugees."

He threw back his handsome head and guffawed until the place rang.

"Who could resist two such lovely ladies in distress!" he chuckled. "It will be as good as a pantomime to see how the two of you get along together. I guess the sparks will soon be flying. Oh well, as long as you keep out of my way when I'm busy, the more the merrier.

"I don't see Maria feeling so hilarious about it however," he went on, referring to the housemaid. "I'd better go up and find her and arrange for two bedrooms to be prepared. Wait in the drawing room and Spadoni will get you anything you want."

Enrico went off, while Spadoni looked expectantly at Carlotta as he led the way to more comfortable surroundings.

"I want no refreshment before dinner," she said, "but I would like that blue-linen dress I left to be washed on my last visit. It's cool and comfortable for mornings in the country. Is your laundress about?"

"Francesca, signorina? Why yes, she is here today. I will send her at once from the laundry."

Carlotta paced about the sumptuous room, a frown marring the perfection of her features. I sensed that my presence here was something she had not bargained for. Yet my right was greater than hers, so she would just have to make the best of it.

Presently Francesca made her appearance, a few garments hanging on her arm.

Plain, plump, and around thirty, she looked old before her time in her black frock and patched apron. She probably left a large family down in some drab Almina tenement to come and do the laundry at the villa, and earn a little extra to make ends meet.

"Ah, you've washed my blue dress I see," Carlotta said.

A look of acute apprehension crossed the woman's face.

"Well, give it to me! Don't stand there like a dummy!"

The laundress looked more afraid than ever.

"'Scuse me, signorina," she said haltingly, "but there was a small accident. I misjudged the heat of the iron."

Frowning, Carlotta snatched the garment and held it up for inspection. There, right on the front of the skirt, was a brown scorch mark.

"You clumsy idiot!" Carlotta stormed. Flinging the dress to the floor, she raised her hand and delivered a resounding slap on the cringing face of the unfortunate servant.

"Stop it!" I remonstrated. "A genuine mistake doesn't give you the right to inflict corporal punishment."

"Hold your tongue, signorina! It is not the first time this fool has made a mistake, as you term it. However, it will certainly be the last at the villa. I may not be mistress here yet, but I know that in this matter your master will endorse me. Collect your wages from Spadoni and don't dare to come back here, ever!"

Francesca's face, all except the red mark, paled. Brokenly, she began to plead. With a workless husband, she was the main support of her family, and though her wage was meager, the left-over food given her by the cook meant the difference between starvation and reasonable existence to her brood.

Carlotta curtly stemmed the flow. "Work *may* be short here in Almina. You should have considered that before and taken more pains to please. Away with you!"

Bursting into tears, the woman fled.

What a vixen Carlotta was, I reflected as I hurried after the retreating figure, making for the seclusion of the laundry.

"What a shame! I'm so sorry," I murmured, placing my hand consolingly on her arm. "I'm sure such harshness never existed in my father's day."

She shook her head. "Never, signorina. I know. I have been coming here for five years. Signor Moravia was a fine man, but after his death everything changed. All the servants were dismissed and new ones set on. All except me, who only comes in three days a week and works for next to nothing. It is the food from the kitchen I took home that my bambini will miss most. Now it will be given to the dog, and they will starve."

"No!" I declared. "I'll help you myself somehow. Tell me

your address, Francesca. In any case, I'd like to talk to you, somewhere private away from here."

She had been coming here during Margaret's brief tragic reign, I reflected, as I reached for the laundry pad and jotted down the address she gave me, afterward tearing out the page. Surely she had picked up some impressions in the way servants do. With luck I might learn something that would establish more clearly whether my half sister had been ill before she contracted the fatal cholera, and what the nature of it was.

"I'll call tomorrow afternoon," I promised.

She summoned a smile. "You are kind, signorina, like the signora my master married. But she was here only a little while then she die of cholera."

My interest quickened. How I longed to question her, but this was neither the place nor time. Even now Enrico might be waiting to show me my room, or Spadoni lurking around, so I only pressed her hand and turned away with a murmured, "Tomorrow afternoon."

Enrico returned to the drawing room shortly after I, looking decidedly grim.

"This confounded war will be the ruination of me," he grumbled. "I have just been in touch with my agent who informs me that all trade with France and Britain has been abruptly severed. That is a body blow, Paris, the center of the perfume industry, having been by far our best customer to date. The fruit might as well rot on the trees, for all the good it will be to us now."

Carlotta laughed. "Don't be so melodramatic, Enrico, *mio!* I cannot see you ever living in poverty. You are far too enterprising. You'll always be one of the top dogs."

"You are right, Carlotta. Now that I've tasted wealth and power I shall never be kicked around by fate again," he said darkly. "What do either of you know of poverty? Carlotta applauded and fawned on as a star, and Lisa cosseted in her Welsh castle all her life with every whim granted! Me, I know it too well."

My glance took in his powerful frame, his handsome face, his piercing, ruthless eyes that seemed to bore through one. Surely he was no mean peasant, dragged up in the gutter. He looked more like a nobleman's son.

"Oh yes," he went on, as though reading my thoughts, "blue blood runs in my veins, though it counted for nothing in my early days. *Mama, mia* was only a serving wench, used by her master for his pleasure and cast off with nothing when I was born. What misery I endured, living by my wits. Starving, thieving, lying. I vowed that one day I would have my revenge on the ruling classes, and especially on the man who had betrayed *mama, mia*. Fortunately, he had given me one asset. My good looks. I've used them to the full as I grew up to get what I wanted. You can imagine how it delights me to see the Fascists in power and the Royalists hunted men. They'll never be allowed to rise again, by heaven!"

I went cold inside as the truth flashed upon me. Carlo's family had been aristocrats. He had been born to wealth and power. Now it was gone, stolen from him and many others like him by as ruthless a sect as Hitler's legions in Germany. Carlo and Angelo were no Mafia villains as I had first surmised, but courageous opponents of this hated regime. As underground resisters they sabotaged vital structures and supplies and would be punished by death if they were caught. Their only help coming from a few staunch supporters like Dr. Crossley, ever ready to afford refuge and medical help even though his own life would be forfeit if he were caught aiding rebels.

At the realization, a warm surge of feeling for David Crossley welled up. British to the core, no patriotic fervor impelled him on as it did with Carlo. He chose this dangerous path freely, no doubt because he, too, despised the Fascists, who murdered and plundered and unleashed the dogs of war.

Gorini's next words filled me with even deeper concern.

"Speaking of hunted men reminds me of something else my agent just told me. A known rebel by name of Angelo Spoletta has been sighted in Almina. We had better all be on guard in case he drifts this way. No doubt he'll be caught before long. In the meantime, it would be safest for you two to keep to the grounds of the villa."

"Never fear for me, Enrico, *mio*," Carlotta declared. "I shall practice my arias in the blessed peace of this place until I bore you."

"So, and what of you Lisa? How will you pass your time?"

Prevarication was useless I decided. Leaving the villa regularly each morning as I would be doing, he would soon find out for himself.

"No need to worry about me," I said cheerfully. "I shall be doing a little clerical work at the hospital most mornings to keep me out of mischief. Dr. Crossley mentioned that it was difficult to find educated people prepared to do voluntary work. I don't mind if it will keep boredom at bay."

He frowned. For a moment I thought he was about to forbid it.

"You surely can't object, the hospital being founded by my father and kept up from the same source! This estate, in fact."

"Oh well, if that's your notion of passing the time. Come to think of it, you might be useful there. You can keep a sharp look out for anything suspicious. I've heard rumors—" He broke off, then added, "I can't myself see such a mealy-mouthed specimen as Crossley having the guts to aid rebels, but one never knows."

My heart swelled in anger. How dare he speak of David Crossley in such terms. He who rode rough shod over everyone to gain his own ends. And actually have the gall to suggest I act the common spy on such a man. The notion filled me with loathing.

It was an effort to keep my emotions from showing plainly on my face, but it had to be done. No gesture or word that might fan his latent suspicions must ever escape me. Any slip of mine could have the most serious effect on the courageous doctor or on dashing, daredevil Carlo.

The two men who in a matter of days had come to mean

more to me than I dared admit, for rebels both, the sword of Democles was poised terrifyingly above their heads.

I breathed a sigh of relief when at that moment Maria appeared to announce that our rooms were ready.

Chapter Eight

Angelo should be warned that he had been spotted, I reflected as I undressed that night. He must take more care and keep well away from the town.

Perhaps hunger had driven him there in the search for food. Somehow I must help him. The best time would be early tomorrow morning. If I set off for the hospital around eight instead of nine, I could hurry to his hideout and contact him before going to my work. That way I was less likely to arouse any suspicion.

So I rose at seven, no hardship in this warm climate, and made my way to the kitchen.

The cook, yawning noisily, had evidently just come on duty.

"You want breakfast, signorina, so early?" she asked in surprise.

"Please. You see I'm just starting a little job at the hospital, but don't bother cooking anything for me. Coffee and something cold will be just fine."

"I make the coffee. You take a tray into the pantry and help yourself, signorina."

This was better than I'd hoped, I reflected, surveying the groaning shelves, and choosing a modest repast for myself.

Recalling Angelo, I slapped a dozen of yesterday's rolls into the bag hanging on my arm, adding salami, some slices of ham, and half-a-dozen peaches. Then picking up my tray, I marched back into the kitchen.

"All ready for you, signorina."

The good-natured woman filled small jugs with coffee and

hot milk and placed them on the tray. I added crockery and cutlery and staggered up to my room with the loot.

I drank the fragrant beverage, ate a couple of rolls and a slice of ham, then wrapped the rest in the napkin and stowed it in my rush bag with the purloined food.

With many a backward glance to make certain that I was not being followed, I sped away, past the hospital gates, past the narrower track that led up to the ruined castle, and onto the wild mountain side.

My suspicions were deepening that it was a meeting place for the Mafia. And having seen Enrico leave there yesterday afternoon, it was a safe bet to assume that he was one of them, probably the local leader, powerful as he was. By his own declaration he hated the rich and high born, so what more natural than that he should lead a gang who battened on all who could be fleeced by extortion and terrorism.

He was also a self-confessed Fascist. A member of the two sects grimly opposed to such as Carlo and David Crossley. A man to beware of indeed.

Presently I reached the vicinity of the cave, where a drift of wood smoke assailed my nostrils. With Angelo's presence in the district suspected, that was too risky.

He knelt outside the cave tending a tiny fire of dry sticks. Perched on stones above it was a blackened tin from which an odor of coffee stole out.

He started up, reaching automatically for his gun as I stepped into view, then relaxed when he recognized me.

I set down the basket.

"I've brought you some food."

He glanced inside. "*Grazie, signorina. Mio, dio,* how good it will taste. Now what of Carlo? Have you heard anything?"

"He's going to be all right in a while. Meantime, he's comfortable. I can't say the same for you though. I have it on good authority that you were spotted in Almina, and somebody gave you away. They'll start hunting you down today."

With an oath he sprang to his feet, snatched the tin from the embers and began to stamp on the glowing twigs with his heavy boots until they were extinguished. Then he kicked the stones aside and proceeded to scatter what debris he could find over the blackened scar.

"Come inside," he murmured, even though, with the coverage of rocks and bushes it was impossible to be spotted here by anyone more than a few yards away.

I followed him in through the flowery curtain and stood while he drank the coffee and began to wolf down the food.

"This rumor of my being seen," he said in between mouthfuls. "I suppose you heard it in your pensione?"

I shook my head. "It was Gorini himself who told me."

"*Mio, dio!* You have been in touch with *him?*"

The truth was simpler than evasion, and he had a right to know how matters stood.

"I was turned out of the pensione yesterday because of an expected party from Naples, so had no option but to take refuge in the Villa Caterina. With the outbreak of war, I'm a virtual prisoner here, worse luck."

"There of all places!" Anger and suspicion made his voice harsh.

"It's perfectly natural," I said, weary by now of explaining my position. "As Lisa Moravia I was born there but banished to Wales. I only came out here to investigate my half sister's sudden death soon after she married Gorini. I suspect he had a hand in it."

"I'll wager he had if he stood to gain anything, but you're no match for a man like Gorini. If he thinks you're probing into the affair—"

"He won't. He regards me as a brash schoolgirl, and it doesn't bother him having me at the villa. In fact, he suggested it."

"Don't let that fool you. The spider's web looks attractive to the fly, but the wretched fly finds himself enmeshed when he wants to escape."

I shivered. The cave felt suddenly cold.

"Better not come here again," he said dourly. "It's not so much I don't trust you, but sooner or later you'd be bound to give yourself, and me, away. In any case, I'm only hanging on here until Carlo's fit to leave hospital and we can make plans and move on."

Warm satisfaction flooded me.

"I can speed that a little at least, since I'm now helping to nurse him. If Dr. Crossley can trust me sufficiently to let me into his top secret shrine, surely you can."

His dourness ebbed a little.

"So! Our trusted contacts do not usually take risks, but in this case I'm surprised he has taken you into his confidence so quickly, living in the Villa Caterina as you do."

I was silent. I had been at the pensione when he took me on, but it was now too late for David Crossley to retract, now that I knew so much about him and his secret hospital.

"In a way his hand was forced," I conceded, "partly by my already knowing half the story through stumbling on you and Carlo, and partly because he was desperate for extra help in the Swordfish Ward. Actually he's a good judge of character, for I'd rather die than betray him. None of you are in the least danger from me, I swear it."

"Not intentionally perhaps, but you're too vulnerable for this game, signorina."

"What goes on in that ruined castle?" I asked to change the subject. "It seems a sinister place, and I saw Gorini leaving it yesterday. Is it the Mafia?"

"Most likely. No one discusses these things openly, nor should you. Shun the place and be ever on your guard at all times, now that you know too much for your own good—and live on a razor edge, so to speak."

I nodded, conscious of the truth of his words, then pushed my way out into the sunlight.

"High time I was on my way to the hospital."

"Take great care when you pass the road that leads to the *castello*," he warned. "If anyone is in sight, stay concealed until all is clear."

"I will."

I was about to hurry away when he clutched my arm with a mumbled, "Listen, signorina!"

I froze, straining my ears. Faintly, from deep in the ravine, away toward the direction of Almina, came the barking of a dog, followed by raised human voices. The resonance of the silent valley sent the sounds floating up, in spite of the distance.

"The hunt has started. They are searching down by the river, fanning out from the town," he muttered, "but they'll never find this cave, halfway up the slope, among the rocks and trees, with no track leading to it."

Probably true. Only pure chance and the half-conscious groans of Carlo had led me to the spot. Only my hasty retreat and the dislodging of a stone had caused Angelo to dash out through the growing curtain, pinpointing their retreat.

"I hope not," I whispered. "Now I must go, but take care."

"Tread carefully so as not to scatter any stones. Sound carries treacherously in the ravine. Take care of Carlo, signorina."

I sped away, never taking my eyes from the ground ahead so that I should make no false move.

How fearfully I glanced up at the gaunt castle as I neared the crossroad. It was quite deserted, so I passed silently on, through the copse, and into the hospital.

The receptionist at the desk greeted me with a look of surprise.

"I'm doing a little clerical work for Dr. Crossley," I said smoothly. "I'll go through to him. He's expecting me."

She smiled. "How kind of you. He is always overworked."

I passed on to David's office. He was alone and glad to see me.

"I'm operating in twenty minutes on a case that came in early this morning via the secret channel. A stab wound. The anesthetist is preparing the theater now. I'll need him of course and Nurse Ponti too, so I'm thankful you can hold the fort for a short time," he said rising. "I'll take you down there now, then she can scrub up with me."

My heart beating faster, I followed him along the passage, through his room and the secret door, and down to the cellars. I had not bargained for being thrown in at the deep end so soon.

Nurse Ponti greeted me in her calm way.

"I've explained the situation," David Crossley said. "Just give Lisa her instructions and follow me into the theater."

"The morning routine is well under way," Nurse Ponti explained. "I've done the surgical dressings on the more pressing cases. The five end patients over there need their washing water, and numbers nine and ten need their bandages changed. As they are well on their way to recovery, I've no qualms about letting you do it. After that you can make coffee for them all, not forgetting the single-room patient. I should be back soon after that, and then we can make all the beds together."

I scarcely heard her last words. The single-room patient was, of course, Carlo. How fortunate that I should be able to speak to him alone about Angelo.

And not only because of Angelo, my racing pulse whispered. I tried hard to ignore it. A rebel and a fugitive, I was mad to look on him through rose-tinted glasses, and the same went for David Crossley, around whose fair head I was in danger of hanging a halo. Danger was their bedfellow, romance a luxury for which they had no time, yet they both evoked something in me that I had never known before. A secret enchantment that threatened to overwhelm me.

Alone in the ward, I brought washing facilities for the five patients pointed out, saying a few cheerful words to each as I spread towels and propped them up. Beyond wide smiles and enthusiastic *salutes*, they said little that I could understand, but helped me enormously by gesture and co-operation.

When I had finished with the two bandage cases, I put away my dressings tray and went into the small side ward.

Carlo was propped up by pillows, but his eyes were closed as though he had dozed off. So I was able to gaze my fill without embarrassment, and almost resented it when the black lashes were abruptly raised and he stared piercingly at me.

"*Buon giorno, signorina*," he said. "What are you doing here?"

"I'm helping out in the mornings. Remember?"

"In my case, Nurse Ponti has forestalled you in her usual efficient manner, so you don't need waste your time on me."

His coolness was like a dash of cold water. Rebuffed, I said tartly, "I know that, and thank heaven I *don't* have to start on a mulish patient like you! The others were both co-operative and appreciative."

His sensitive mouth creased then. How devilishly engaging he looked with his white teeth showing and his brown eyes deepening to warmth. How on earth could I be expected to harden my heart against him?

"I glanced in merely to pass on something regarding Angelo, but of course if you don't want to hear it, I'll go."

"Angelo!" His hand shot out and clutched mine as though he feared I would carry out my threat. "Is he all right?"

"Physically in great shape, but none too safe where his freedom is concerned. Someone spotted him in Almina and gave him away."

"*Mio, dio!* How do you know this?"

"Enrico Gorini mentioned it, and warned me not to stray far from the villa. He little knows the truth." I smiled nervously.

"That villain's name is never off your tongue!" Carlo growled. "What are you doing at the villa? You said you were at the Pensione Antonio."

"I was turned out and had nowhere else to go. The circumstance proved lucky for Angelo. I was able to go to the cave and warn him that the hunt was on for him. Surely that proves I'm a hundred per cent behind you."

"It also proves you're foolishly reckless, and none of us have any right to involve a mere child like you in such a dangerous game," he said gravely. "At the same time, your help has been invaluable to Angelo and me. I have to thank you for that."

The pressure of his hand on mine, which he still held, was warm and sincere. Tingling all over, I hastily pulled away. Emotionally, I was no child.

"We've none of us any options," I said unevenly. "Fate has thrown us together and decreed I can't leave until the cessation of hostilities. I had reason to suspect and hate Gorini before ever I set eyes on him. Nothing has happened to change that view, so anyone opposed to him and his regime is a friend of mine. I'm just happy to be of help in a small way to any of you, especially Dr. Crossley. His risk is colossal."

Carlo nodded. "Get me patched up and out of here as quickly as you can. Angelo won't leave until I can go with him I guess, but now, the hunt is on he's a potential danger to the hospital and our good friends here. I'd rather die than bring trouble on them."

And it could be closer than he realized, I reflected, recalling Gorini's suspicions. What would Carlo say if he knew that Gorini expected me to act the spy?

"My instructions from Nurse Ponti were to make coffee for you all," I said, to change the subject, "so I'll be off to the kitchen. Back in ten minutes."

All the main ward patients tried to inveigle me into lingering with them in their limited communication, but I merely smiled on them all and hurried back to Carlo with his beverage.

He had scarcely finished drinking when Nurse Ponti's calm voice carried through from the main ward. Our confidences were at an end.

I took his cup.

"I must go, but I'll see you tomorrow I expect."

"Be careful," he murmured. "Remember there are spies everywhere. Keep away from the cave, but if by any chance you should see Angelo, tell him to get away while the going's good without waiting for me. I'll make my way to Swordfish N on my discharge and meet him there. He'll know what you mean."

I walked on air from his room. At last he seemed to trust me.

Chapter Nine

Carlotta's presence at lunch proved a blessing in that it took some of Gorini's attention from me. He merely asked how the morning had gone and if I'd heard or seen anything suspicious, then turned to his more voluble guest.

I scarcely heard what they said. My mind was on the unfortunate Francesca and her brood. I had promised to call with food this afternoon, and besides I wanted to talk to her, yet must not arouse my host's suspicions.

Keep to the estate, he had said. Well, that was large enough to swallow me up and hide my movements, if I took care when leaving the place. But it was a long walk to the town and all the way back up the hill. If only I had some form of transport.

"I suppose there doesn't happen to be a cycle about the place?" I asked during a lull in the conversation. "Cycling round the estate would give me some fresh air and exercise."

Enrico laughed. "What would I do with a cycle? I have my comfortable car and my excellent horse to carry me. There's an aging mare in the stables if you ride. She could do with some exercise I dare say."

"Of course I ride, and in as rough country as this having lived all my life in the Welsh hills."

"There you are then. Problem settled. How about you Carlotta? I could hire a steady mount for you."

She raised her hands in horror.

"Are you mad, Enrico! I should fall off in five minutes. I'll be quite happy left to my own devices when you're busy, thank you."

Thank heaven for that, I thought. Company was the last thing I desired on my secret comings and goings.

When Spadoni came in with the dessert, Enrico ordered Seraphina to be prepared for me, and after the meal was over, I made my way round to the stables at the back.

Beppo, the stable lad, had her ready. In halting English he assured me that she would give no trouble if treated gently. I had no riding habit with me, but in this summer heat, my linen slacks were adequate, and I rode off in high spirits, not round the estate, but out of a side gate not overlooked by the house.

Afternoon heat lay heavily on the land as Seraphina jogged sedately through the copse and past the hospital. A nervous glance up at the castle assured me that no one was about, and I rounded the bend and took the downward road as quietly as possible.

The sea of red roofs clustered by the river bank presently leveled into the town, now drowsing in the afternoon siesta. Near-deserted streets showed starkly the dirt and decay that lay over all. The broken steps of a crumbling church on which ragged urchins played. An open door showing a glimpse of a dark interior in which sat a peasant woman in black shelling brown beans, a barefoot girl in patched frock filling her jar from the trickle of water that came from a spout in a wall.

Where could I buy food? I wondered, noting the shuttered shops.

A mound of rotting vegetables and fruit led me up a side street to a market, now almost finished for the day. The few stallkeepers left were packing their remaining produce into baskets, prior to departure. They stared at me in surprise.

With a few words of halting Italian, eked out by gestures, I managed to fill my straw bag with misshapen tomatoes, wilting lettuce, and left-over fruit. Then from a dark little adjoining trattoria I bought bread, pasta, salami, and cheese.

A dingy Sicilian cart and pony were hitched outside. Could I leave my mare there too for a short time? I asked.

"*Si, si, signorina,*" the curly-haired proprietor beamed.

So I tied Seraphina alongside, and my now heavy basket on my arm, I left the side street and the stinking pile of refuse.

Number 10, Via Barletta, was Francesca's address. A grubby urchin offered to guide me there. He turned along a narrow alley running steeply down to the river. Dark and sunless, the tall dwellings closed in on either side of the alley, reeking of apathy and decay. A few pitiful attempts at decoration in the form of wilting plants straggling from cans on the rickety iron balconies, in no way hid the crumbling stucco and peeling woodwork all around.

Number 10 was a little less dingy than its neighbors. The step was clean, the pavement swept. I dropped a few coins into the extended palm of my guide and clattered the knocker on the handleless door.

Francesca opened it almost immediately, as though she had been waiting. She drew me inside, explaining that her husband and older children were out looking for work.

"Only the bambino here," she added, indicating the child crawling around the floor in company with a mangy dog.

Even in the dim light that filtered through the half-closed shutters I could see the rickety bed left little space for the broken bench and table. There seemed to be no other furniture.

Her glance was fixed on my bulging bag with painful eagerness.

"This was all I could get in the market," I said, spilling the contents on the table. "The shops were closed."

"It is the siesta, signorina, but this is a feast. We eat well tonight."

She broke off a crust of bread and began to nibble it as though very hungry as she stowed the rest away in a wall cupboard.

"Please sit." She indicated the bench and joined me on its unyielding surface. I plunged immediately into my questions, the sooner to leave this squalor behind.

"You remember Margaret, the lady who came to the villa when Signore Moravia was dying?"

"*Si, si!* The villa was left to her, then Signore Gorini pounce like a tarantula. He seemed to cast a spell on her."

"I guessed as much. She was my half sister you know."

Francesca tut-tutted. "Better if she had not come here. Better if *you* had not come, signorina."

"Better indeed, but now I'm trapped too by this wretched war. But I wanted to ask about her health. Tell me everything you can remember about her, Francesca. That was my reason for coming to Calabria—to find out the truth of her death."

Francesca bit her lip. "Better not to probe, signorina. You do not know Calabria. I do."

I clenched my hands. "Listen, Francesca. Not only have I been robbed of my birthright, but my dearest relative has been snatched away from me under highly suspicious circumstances. How can you expect me to ignore all that, while I'm kept kicking my heels here?"

"You will not make trouble for me if I talk?" she asked fearfully. "Signore Gorini is powerful, and bad."

I shook my head. "Of course I shan't implicate you. You have troubles enough. But I particularly want to know what happened to change Margaret so quickly from a healthy, well-balanced woman to a sick and fearful one. I have good reason to believe she was ill *before* the cholera epidemic struck. Is that so?"

Francesca nodded. "She change while they are away on honeymoon. They come back here early because she is sick."

"But what was this illness?"

The laundry maid shrugged, then rubbed her sagging stomach. "She sick most days, and not eat much. Signore Gorini pretend to be sorry. He make her stay in bed. He carry up her food and sit with her, but he not really sorry."

I frowned. It sounded totally out of character for him to fetch and carry trays when he had servants to do it for him.

"Didn't he call a doctor in to find out the cause of the trouble?"

"No, signorina. He say it is the rich food and hot climate of Calabria that upset her. He say she get used to it. Then the cholera epidemic start. Signore Gorini say she have the cholera, but he does not call Dr. Crossley, who always looked after Signore Moravia. No, he bring a strange doctor from Naples."

How extremely convenient that outbreak had proved for Gorini, giving cast-iron immunity against suspicion which otherwise might have been aroused.

I now had an absolute conviction that a crime had been committed. Probably some insidious poison had been introduced into Margaret's food from the very beginning, and the dosage stepped up in the dishes on the trays he so zealously carried up to her on their return to the villa.

I realized poor Margaret must have guessed when it was too late. But how had she managed to get my letter posted?

"Did the signora ever ask you to post a letter for her?" I asked. "An air mail letter to England?"

"*Si, si, signorina,*" Francesca answered.

My lips hardened. What a score I had to settle with the master of the villa if the chance ever came my way.

"I'll try to come again," I promised as I left, "although it is difficult. I've been ordered to keep to the grounds."

She shook her head in commiseration. "It is bad, having to live in the villa, under the shadow of such a man. Do not endanger yourself for me, signorina."

I collected Seraphina and set off back.

The mare took the hill slowly and I saw no reason to rush her. It was so pleasant now that the sinking sun had lost its ferocity. I was ambling along, deep in thought, when an opulent car flashed past, leaving a cloud of dust behind.

In it was Enrico Gorini, with Carlotta beside him.

My heart sank. So he would know I had disregarded his orders to keep to the grounds. Why had he not stopped to remonstrate with me there and then. Surely he had recognized me.

Undoubtedly. He was waiting for me when I rode into the stable area at the back, a black frown on his face.

"So! I advise you to keep to the grounds for your own good and what notice do you take of it?" he growled.

"I refuse to be cooped up like a prisoner!" I retorted. "It's bad enough my being kept away from Wales indefinitely without losing my liberty as well. I have to go out to the hospital most mornings so why not a ride in the afternoon if I choose?"

"You appeared to be returning from Almina, where the outlaw was seen. Why go there?"

"Because I care more about Francesca than you do," I said heatedly. "That laundry work was all that kept her family from starvation. It was monstrous to penalize her so harshly for one mistake, on the whim of a guest."

He stared at me. "You appear to know a great deal about the woman and her family. If you are to remain under my roof I will not have you mixing with such trash. I suppose you acted the Lady Bountiful, doling out alms as in your feudal Wales. Well, that is not the way things are run in Calabria. The peasants are poles apart from those in my position."

"If I choose to take her a meal occasionally, I see no reason for you to object. You've no lawful rights over me as you had over poor Margaret," I added recklessly. "What madness possessed her to marry you I can't imagine."

He shrugged.

"Charming sentiments from one to whom I offer hospitality."

"Only because you feel obliged to. Because you cheated me out of what should have been mine. Because you mesmerized Margaret until she was like wax in your hands, and thereby sealed her own fate."

Immediately, I regretted it. He was too dangerous a man to bait. Too unscrupulous to show so plainly that I suspected him of having brought about my half sister's death.

He just stood scowling, saying nothing. Thinking out the best way of dealing with me, perhaps, and effectively stopping me from seeing Francesca again.

Then he turned and stalked off without a word, leaving me feeling uneasy for the luckless laundry maid more than for myself. She was so much more dispensable.

Oddly, he seemed to have entirely dismissed the episode at

dinner. Far from ignoring me, he pointedly drew me into the conversation to the obvious annoyance of Carlotta.

Even when the meal was over and I would gladly have escaped to my room, he insisted on my joining them in the ornate salon, with its gilt furniture and painted ceiling.

"In these remote places we must all do what we can in the way of entertainment," he said. "Carlotta, of course, has her superb voice. Mine is less remarkable but passable. Now what of little Lisa? An accompanist on the piano would be a real asset. Do you by any chance play?"

"Not well enough to suit such a professional as Signorina Mancini," I declared, gazing with awe at the white expanse of the grand piano.

"Do let her go to bed," Carlotta snapped. "We shall enjoy our evening much more alone than with a gauche little schoolgirl hanging around."

But Enrico only laughed. An imp of perversity seemed to have gripped him. Why was he teasing her? Was he growing tired of her proprietary attitude? Was he contrasting her mature allurements, verging on the point of overblown, with my coltish charm? Or was there something more sinister in his mind, such as wanting to wear down my resistance? Whatever his motivation, it was doomed to disappointment, with two such men as David Crossley and Carlo Valachi in orbit.

He took me firmly by the shoulders and propelled me to the piano stool.

"Now play some little air. Anything you know well, and we shall not mock you."

In spite of Carlotta's patent annoyance, or perhaps because of it, I fingered the keys to savor their rich response, then drifted into a haunting Welsh tune that came almost mechanically.

Enrico actually applauded and demanded more.

I obliged, delighting in the dulcet tone of the instrument in spite of my nervousness. But when later he suggested my accompanying Carlotta I rose and made my escape.

His sudden blandishments I distrusted instinctively; they made me far more uneasy than his anger.

Chapter Ten

Again I did not wait for a leisurely breakfast with Gorini and Carlotta the following morning, but had rolls and coffee sent into the dining salon earlier.

I ate all three rolls with enjoyment. If either Francesca or Angelo were to be helped out with food today, I should have to buy again, I reflected as I went out into the cooler morning air and on my way to the hospital.

David Crossley was giving instructions to a junior doctor when I entered his office. He dismissed the young Italian and turned to me, his serious face lighting up with that rare smile that went straight to my heart.

"Good of you to come so early, Lisa. It's quite a walk from Almina."

"Oh I didn't have to come that far," I confessed, unsure of how he would take the news of my move. "Having been turned out of the pensione, I'm now living at the Villa Caterina."

"What!" He rose to his feet, his smile changing to concern. "I'm sorry to hear it."

"From my point of view do you mean? Oh things could be worse. I have every luxury, and though Enrico Gorini is not my idea of congenial company, the opera singer Carlotta Mancini is also visiting. She dominates the scene, and takes his attention from me."

"I was thinking more of the underground movement, and the hospital in particular," he said somberly. "The danger of detection is ever present."

"I know, and believe me, Dr. Crossley, I'll guard your secret to the death. Have no fears on that score."

He laughed shortly. "My dear child, you haven't the faintest idea what you're up against. If the Fascists so much as suspected that we were working against them, aiding and sheltering wounded resisters, they'd be down on us immediately and ransack the place for evidence, or even manufacture some. It would be the end of our work here and no doubt of me too. Gorini, I suspect, has climbed to his present position by dabbling in every dirty racket going, including the Mafia and Fascism. So he is to be doubly feared. To have you living there and coming here frequently, under whatever pretext, is walking on a razor's edge."

I nodded, horribly aware that Gorini already harbored vague distrust of both the hospital and its chief.

"But I've nowhere else to go, and I should go crazy just mooning around the villa and estate, while you need help so desperately. Don't say I must stop coming, please, Dr. Crossley!"

He sighed. "Having started, it might arouse Gorini's suspicions if you suddenly stopped. There seems no other course than to continue for the time being until you can think of a legitimate excuse to end it."

To stop coming. To see his dear face no more. To be barred from helping my thrilling Carlo and other brave men in dire need. How could I face it.

"Is it possible for me to live at the hospital?" I asked in a rush. "I should be able to give a lot more help then, and not have daily contact with Gorini."

Sadly he shook his head. "That would be drawing you into danger up to the neck. I could never permit you to take the full risk that we few in the movement take, my dear child."

Though I clenched my hands hard, I could not stop the tears of frustration from rolling down my cheeks. What a thing of conflict life had suddenly become.

"Don't cry," he said softly. "Dear, dear Lisa."

His arms were about me, warm and comforting. My face was pressed against his white coat, where the pocket pens bit into it, and yet the hurt was sweet. I turned to him as to the father I had never known.

Presently he dried my eyes.

"For the moment we'll say no more on the matter. Sister Casini will be waiting for her morning summons to discuss cases. She is not in the movement, so we must give her no cause to suspect that all is not aboveboard. Come, sit down at this desk and act the efficient private secretary. It's fortunate for our purpose that my last part-time one has recently left. Sooner or later I'm bound to find another, but under the circumstances it's extremely difficult to get hold of the right person. I'm having to do my most important work myself. The rest I send out to the general office.

I followed him into a poky cubbyhole that opened off his spacious room. Lined with cupboards and filing cabinets, it accommodated merely a desk and chair besides.

"Typing is not one of my accomplishments, I'm afraid," I said, eyeing the machine on the desk.

"No matter. Take off the cover and pretend. Any good at figures?"

"Top of the class in math."

"Splendid. Just check these figures then while Sister is with me. Afterward you can go down to Swordfish Ward."

As soon as I was composed at the desk and checking through the papers he put before me, he returned to his own office and rang for Sister Casini, purposely leaving the door ajar so that she could catch a glimpse of me working and take me at face value.

She was with him about fifteen minutes. They spoke in Italian too rapid for me to comprehend anything but a stray word or two, and when she rose to leave she glanced in on me with a smile and friendly, *"Buon giorno, signorina."*

As soon as the door closed firmly behind her, he signaled for me to come out.

"Can you find your own way down, Lisa? I have already seen the patients in Swordfish and Sister Casini has an urgent case she wants me to look at."

"Surely, Doctor, now I know just where the secret springs are on both sides of the cupboard partition."

"Be extremely careful when you're leaving. If I'm not in my office, just go quietly off as though you were leaving work here. And remember, Swordfish and the movement are something you've never heard of."

I nodded, deeply conscious now of the precariousness of my position.

Nurse Ponti was glad to see me, and this time I was able to help her with a little more confidence as we went the rounds together, first doing surgical dressings and then making beds.

"Now that only leaves the side ward, and then it will be time for coffee. Come."

"How is Carlo this morning?" I asked, having wanted to ask it all morning.

She raised her eyebrows. "Names are never used, Lisa. He is patient number twelve, and his progress is excellent. He has a remarkable physique."

I glowed inwardly, telling myself that my interest was so personal because I had been the means of getting him here in the first place and perhaps saving his life. I was not to be fooled. I knew it went deeper than that.

He looked less pale, but bored. At our entry his expression brightened.

"When are you going to let me out of this bed, nurse?" he demanded.

"Probably this morning if your temperature is behaving well, now that Lisa is here to assist. I could not have spared the time on my own."

His glance slid to me. Like warm dark velvet it curled sensuously about me, leaving a tingling in its wake that I could not repress.

It persisted all through our administrations. The touch of his firm, sun-bronzed flesh did devastating things to my undisciplined emotions, so that I was glad of the presence of Nurse Ponti.

At the close she produced a crutch.

"Out you get, since your temperature is more docile than you. You may practice hobbling round your room for ten minutes or so. Stay and assist him, Lisa. We don't want him keeling over and undoing all the good work."

She helped him out of bed, tucked the crutch under his arm and motioned me to his other side.

"Lend him your support. He's pretty groggy still. I'll be back presently." She hurried away.

"Once again I depend on you, signorina," he said, wrapping his free arm round my shoulders while I clutched him round the waist.

His progress was awkward and halting at first until he found a measure of co-ordination. Then, stumbling less as he hobbled slowly round and round the bed, he said, "How goes your stay at the Villa Caterina?"

"Stormily. I was practically forbidden to leave the place, but rebelled. One asset, I'm allowed the use of an aging mare, so movement is facilitated. I'm able to ride down into Almina and back much faster. I'm trying to help a laundry woman unfairly dismissed."

In a few words I explained about Francesca, her out-of-work husband and hungry brood.

"Poverty is rife in Calabria, unfortunately."

"The point is, she was at the villa during Margaret's brief stay. My half sister, who came out when my father was dying, fell under Gorini's spell and married him. Within weeks she was dead. The cholera outbreak was blamed, but both Francesca and I know she was ill before then. Having Francesca confirm my suspicions convinces me that Gorini only wanted the estate and Margaret out of the way as soon as possible."

"Typical of the fellow," Carlo said grimly. "And, by the way, this Francesca. If she suspects anything against him and is liable to talk, she'd better watch out. Gorini takes few chances where his own well being is concerned."

I bit my lip, acutely worried on her account, and regretting my outburst yesterday. Had I made things even more difficult for her. I must contact her as soon as possible and warn her to tread warily.

Feeling my tenseness, Carlo paused. "Terrible luck, your getting drawn into all this intrigue, and now being trapped at the villa for the duration. You're not tough enough for such danger. One day I hope to get even with him though. The list of scores to settle grows ever greater."

"Don't do anything desperate and dangerous when you leave here," I said impulsively. "Your leg won't be normal for some time. And with Gorini's gang on the lookout for Angelo, it would be madness to linger in that cave. You must both get away as he intends."

Carlo grinned. "So the little signorina now gives the orders, does she! Listen, Lisa, *mia*, every waking and sleeping moment of life for men of the resistance movement is filled with risk and danger. We accept it. But I'll take care, of course," he added, pressing my shoulder reassuringly where his hand rested on it.

He was hobbling a little more confidently by the time Nurse Ponti returned, and she was well pleased.

"Rest now, and later you may try on your own," she said. "Run and make coffee, Lisa, and take it round, while I write up the case sheets."

The morning sped by until it was time for me to leave and prepare for lunch. I could not afford to antagonize Gorini further.

As it happened, neither he nor Carlotta were in for the meal. I enjoyed the rissotto all the more, and then sought out Beppo, the stable lad, who lived above his charges, to prepare Seraphina for me.

Already the animal knew me. She whinnied softly and nuzzled my hand for the sugar I had brought her. Soon I was off, cantering smartly along on the easy, downward gradient.

The town reached, I made my way toward the market as being the only place to buy food during the siesta hours. But the left-over fruit had been of poor quality, so when I noticed an old fellow dozing in his shop doorway down a side street, I turned Seraphina that way.

He sat on a broken chair, a handkerchief covering his eyes, snoring gently. Behind him in the dark interior I could see great sausages hanging in profusion and shelves stocked with other provisions.

A soft growl from the cur at the old man's feet alerted him. He whipped off the handkerchief, rose stiffly to his feet, and with a gesture, invited me to enter.

I hitched my mount to a post and followed him in, staring about at the sacks of cereals, mounds of cheese, and unfamiliar packets and tins.

He spoke no English, but I pointed to the hefty loaves on the counter, the sausages, cheese, and packets of *biscotti*.

Beaming, the old fellow filled my bag and named the price. I handed over the precious lire with a qualm at the way my stock was dwindling, then leaving Seraphina drinking the water kindly given her, went off toward the river.

Nothing stirred in the narrow alley of Via Barletta, sunk in deep shade cast by the tall houses. This time I was kept waiting longer after I rang the bell, but at last the door was opened by a plump Italian, disheveled and bleary-eyed, who had evidently been disturbed from his siesta.

"So sorry to get you out of bed," I apologized, hoping he could speak English like his wife. "I thought the children might like these biscuits. Is Francesca about?"

"No, signorina. She went up to the hospital this morning, to ask if she could do some washing for them. She said she would be back soon. She did not come to make the spaghetti. We had nothing to eat."

"These biscuits will be welcome then. Perhaps they were glad of Francesca's services and gave her an immediate job," I consoled. "She'll probably come back with both food and good news of work."

As I rode back up the hill, nagging doubts gnawed at me. Francesca knew that I worked in the hospital each morning. Why had she not contacted me?

I reached the top of the hill and paused, still dogged by nameless uneasiness. On Seraphina's willing back it would take only a few minutes to call at the hospital and find out for myself if Francesca had indeed obtained work there. How glad I should be to see her occasionally and know her fears of near starvation were no longer threatening her.

So I turned left and into the now familiar white gates, and after hitching the mare to a post, stepped into the cool waiting room, now empty of patients.

The secretary-receptionist glanced up in surprise from her desk.

"Signorina Moravia! Are you on additional afternoon duties now?"

I smiled. "Not yet. I merely called to ask you if a certain Francesca Grimondi came in this morning, seeking work in the laundry, and if she was successful."

The receptionist frowned in concentration. "No," she said decisively. "We had our usual quota of outpatients, but no one seeking work of any kind."

"You are certain of that?" The nagging doubt within me mounted.

Signora Monisi nodded. "No one contacted me at any rate. It is possible that if she were familiar with the layout of the hospital, she could have gone directly to the laundry to make enquiries there. You could ask if you care to. You know where it is?"

I nodded. It was round at the back, the entrance not far from the dispensary.

"I'll do that," I said, turning away.

The steamy laundry, with its drying ground full of flapping white sheets, had ceased its frenzied morning round, and now lay quiet until the next burst of activity. Only the head laundry maid was left, making out a list of cleaning materials required.

To my enquiry she shook her head. "No one applied for work this morning, signorina. It would have been useless. We have all the hands we need."

Thanking her mechanically, I stepped outside, the doubts within me now a rising flood.

Where was Francesca? What had happened to her? I wondered, as I set off to find Angelo and tell him of Carlo's progress.

It was fortunate that Seraphina was steady and docile, for I exercised very little control as I took to the hills and we picked our way along the tortuous paths. Well before the cave I tethered the animal, just in case any stray searcher noticed her and came to investigate.

Angelo was delighted to see me, and not only for the sake of the food.

"*Mio, dio!* I shall die of boredom if this continues much longer," he groaned. "Holed up here like a fox with the hounds on his track. What news of Carlo?"

"Good news. He's up, and his leg is doing so well that he'll be joining you in a few days."

"Bravo. Did you notice any activity around, or have they abandoned the search for me I wonder."

"Quiet as the grave," I said.

"So! Maybe that accident this morning finished it and they'll seek no further."

"Accident?"

"Well, it sounded like it. Early this morning I had just stepped outside the cave to stretch my cramped limbs when I heard a faint scream, some distance off, followed by a crashing noise like rocks and boulders tumbling down into the ravine. The slight morning mist rising from the river prevented me seeing any distance, and of course I dived back under cover. I heard nothing else though. Most likely it was a lone searcher got too near the edge of a sudden drop. I reckon he'd be killed outright, but could not put the cause in jeopardy by going to investigate."

"It's an ill wind . . ." I said. "If it's put paid to the search, it's done you and Carlo a good turn."

He nodded. "Odd, though. The scream sounded as thin as a woman's."

My heart seemed to stop beating.

"From which direction did it come?" I asked when I could find my voice.

He pointed up and away toward the ruined castle.

"Then it could have been Francesca," I whispered, white-faced.

"Francesca? Who is she?"

I quickly told him everything. "Moreover, Francesca now seems to be missing. Her husband says she left first thing this morning to go up to the hospital looking for laundry work. She never arrived there, nor had she returned home by mid-afternoon."

Angelo shrugged. "That explains the scream. You will never see the unfortunate signora again. She is just another victim of the Gorini gang."

"But how could Gorini or any of his followers know she would be on the hill this morning, since she had ceased coming up to the villa?" I asked in horror.

"They could not know. It was just one of those tricks of fate that played right into their hands. Immediately Gorini suspected her of being a menace to him by spreading doubts about his late wife's death, he would alert all his local henchmen to look out for and get rid of her. They congregate in the old *castello* and could easily have been out looking for me. Instead they spotted her, hustled her up to the *castello*, questioned her, then hustled her out again and flung her down into the ravine along with scattered boulders."

I started up. "God in heaven! In that case she may well be alive, lying terribly injured somewhere. We can't just leave her to die! Surely we must search for her!"

Grim-faced, he grasped my arm and pulled me down again.

"Softly, softly, signorina. You do not know the Mafia. They would not be so stupid as to throw her into the ravine alive in case she lived to tell the tale. A knife in the back, that is their way. If her body is ever found down among the tangle of undergrowth and rocks, the stab wound may well be obliterated. If not, no one will dare to come out into the open with questions. Violent deaths in Calabria cause little comment. They happen too frequently."

I crouched there as though turned to stone. That mangled body could well have been mine. I had better think twice before crossing swords with Gorini again, by showing too clearly that I considered him responsible for Margaret's death. Cunning demanded cunning. Secret planning and underground work in the manner of Carlo and Angelo.

"It seems awful that they can get away with such crimes," I said fiercely.

"Not always, signorina." The set lines of his face belied the softness of his voice. *What had he in mind?*

"Do you carry that invaluable notebook and pencil, signorina?" he asked while I was still pondering.

Silently I produced it from my rush bag.

With concentration he wrote, filling a small page, then tearing it out, handed it back to me.

"Will you give this to Carlo when you see him tomorrow?"

"Of course. May I ask what it says since I don't read Italian?"

"You would not understand even if you could read it. It is in code. The only way we ever send written messages. It is to the effect that this vicinity is getting too hot to linger in. I shall be off before dawn tomorrow. When Carlo is fit again he can join me at the appointed place. The hospital dispenser will arrange transport for him."

Slowly I nodded. "It is better that way. It would be a great strain on his healing wound climbing down to this cave."

But what a void it would leave in my life. Not seeing him again, or even Angelo, for in a curious way I had become attached to him, because he was Carlo's friend.

Chapter Eleven

I had not been in bed very long that night and was still awake when a frantic pealing of the front-door bell, followed by furious barking of the dog, roused me completely. What on earth was happening to cause so much commotion?

Heavy running footsteps passed my door. Spadoni going down from his upper bedroom to open up and find out what was going on, no doubt. Then suddenly I realized that the room seemed lighter than normal, and sliding out of bed, I rushed to the open window and peered out.

From across the gardens, away down the slopes where the citrus groves lay fragrant with blossom, a lurid glow was lighting the sky. It seemed to grow brighter as I gazed. The extensive buildings where the bergamot fruit was stored and processed lay alongside, I recalled. Surely they were on fire, and that was the cause of the stir.

As I stood hesitant, the household sprang to life below. Spadoni and another man ran round from the front door to view what could be seen of the conflagration from this distance. The cook joined them, and then Gorini, cursing and roaring angrily for the stable lad.

Beppo came at the run, bleary-eyed, barefoot and half dressed, clearly roused from sleep.

"Start the car immediately!" Gorini ordered. "There's no time to lose in getting down there if the whole lot isn't to go up in flames. I'll fetch my gun. It could be arson, and if I catch a glimpse of the scoundrels, they'll pay for it."

He dashed into the house, to return within minutes. By this time Beppo had the car waiting. They all piled in and set off, the dog with them, presumably to help track down any miscreants.

Recalling Angelo's dour expression and cryptic remark yesterday when he felt certain Francesca had been murdered, uneasiness flooded me. If he had started the fire in revenge, he might not yet be very far away. With a car and a dog on his trail he could easily be caught.

Consumed with anxiety, it was now impossible to return to bed, or even remain in my room. Hastily I dressed in the few garments necessary in this warm southern climate, slipped on sandals and opened my door, to find a petulant-looking Carlotta outside.

"*Mio, dio!* Will someone tell me what is going on?" she exclaimed. "I came here for peace and quiet, not bedlam. Where is Enrico? Not in his room."

"He's gone down to the citrus groves," I said. "Some of the buildings seem to be on fire. The household was roused by one of the men from down there."

She spread her hands in horror.

"A fire! *Mio, dio!* Is it likely to spread this way?"

I shrugged impatiently.

"Hardly. What wind there is blows the other way. However, I'm going down to see for myself. As for you, signorina, you had better go back to your room since you'd be no help there." I glanced at her diaphanous draperies in scorn. If she had been anticipating an amorous session with Enrico, she was going to be disappointed.

She shuddered. "Nothing would tempt me down there amidst the smoke and heat. Enrico should have left it to the servants. Let us hope he comes to no harm." Haughtily she turned and stalked back to the safety of her bedroom.

I sped downstairs. In the turmoil the front door had been left wide open. I dashed through and round to the back, and now the light in the sky down by the citrus groves was growing more livid.

In the evening stillness, shouts could be heard from that direction, and the barking of the dog. Had they perhaps sighted

Angelo, I wondered with sinking heart. Up here all was un-
usually quiet—the entire household, with the exception of Carlotta, was down at the fire without doubt.

Overhead there was a new moon. It cast very little light, but
sufficient to show the main path leading down through the
formal Italian garden with its geometrical beds and clipped low
hedges and the fountain playing in the center.

Then my heart seemed to stop. Something darted between
the cover of one riotous rose bush to the next, unaware perhaps
of my silent approach in my soft sandals.

I stood rooted, unable either to retreat or advance. My voice,
when it came, was a mere croak.

"Who's there?"

There was a cautious movement. A blurred face peered out,
then a man strode swiftly across, taking the low hedge in one
athletic bound.

"Signorina Lisa, by all that's wonderful," he murmured
hoarsely.

It was Angelo.

I grasped his arm. "I guessed it might be you exacting revenge
when the alarm was raised," I whispered, "but what in heaven's
name are you doing here? Gorini's looking for you with gun,
dog, and car. He'll kill you for certain if he catches you. You
ought to be well on your way out of it by now."

He actually grinned. "I'm safer up near the villa than anywhere at the moment. I figured the fire would rouse the entire
household and draw them down there, so slipped away and hid
in the gardens before it was discovered. What I need is a horse,
to aid my escape across country. I was just about to look for
the stables. Now you can show me the way."

"Follow me," I whispered, safe in the knowledge that Beppo
had gone with the others.

We reached the outbuildings. Would the door be locked? I
wondered anxiously. If so, I should have to waste precious time
searching for the key up in Beppo's loft.

By a stroke of luck it opened at a touch. "Use your torch
and make as little noise as possible," I whispered. "Signorina

Mancini is still about the villa, but her room faces the other way."

His beam of light flicked along the stalls. Only two horses were in occupation. Seraphina, drowsily peaceful, and Enrico's splendid black mount, Tarantula.

"Take the mare," I whispered. "She's docile and steady."

"Reason enough for not taking her," he chuckled. "I am in a hurry. The black will suit my purpose better."

"But that's Enrico's special mount. He'll be furious."

"Better and better. He'll carry me through the night to safety then fetch a good price for the cause. I know just where to dispose of him without trouble. They'll change his appearance so much his own mother wouldn't recognize him."

While he spoke he was busy with saddle and bridle. Tarantula rolled his eyes defiantly at first, but recognizing the touch and the voice of a strong man, soon steadied down.

Angelo led the beast outside, mounted, then touched my cheek in farewell.

"*Arrivederci, signorina,* and *grazie.* Give Carlo my note. And beware of Gorini, a member of both the Mafia and the Fascists."

With a final wave he rode off into the night, the opposite way from where the fire burned, toward the desolate hills.

When all was quiet I found myself shivering with nervous reaction. But it was dangerous to linger here. As I had announced my intention of going down to the scene of excitement some time ago to Carlotta, I had better get down there with all speed.

I softly closed the stable door and sped off, back through the gardens and to the extensive range of buildings down by the plantations.

The scene was as lurid as a film set. The building most affected was the fruit storage house. It blazed furiously and had evidently been written off, for the fire fighters were concentrating their efforts on the adjoining building, already well alight, in an effort to stop it spreading.

I recognized Beppo and Spadoni. The others were the plantation hands who were housed in a row of low shacks a short distance away. Of Enrico there was no sign.

"Where is Signore Gorini?" I asked of Spadoni as he stood directing water from a hose onto the most dangerous looking of the flames.

"Looking for the scoundrels who started it," he grunted. "If he finds them, they'll wish they had never been born. *Dio, mio,* this building looks like going the way of the first. Come on you lazy louts! Turn more water this way. As for you, signorina, now you're here you can help my wife fetch up buckets of water to deal with stray outbreaks."

The plump cook came puffing up now, hair hanging down her back, smoke begriming her cheeks, a laden bucket in her hands. I seized it and hurried to where a tongue of flame shot through a low window, while she went back to the well for more.

Whatever my feelings about the fire, I must make an outward show of trying to quench it, I reflected as I dashed the contents of my bucket at the window and smothered that particular flame.

Soon after, Gorini's car swept up, and his scowling face showed that he had had no success in his search. That was not surprising, since the car would have kept him to the roads, while Angelo was speeding safely away over the hills.

He stood for a moment surveying the damage, Spadoni at his side.

"The storage house is past saving, signore, but the rest we are getting under control," Spadoni said. "We are lucky things are no worse. The buildings are tinder dry and without prompt measures would all have been reduced to ashes."

"Get on then, man," Gorini growled. "This is no time for slackening off."

He himself seized a hose from one of the men and set to with a will. His return seemed to galvanize them all to greater efforts, and within another half hour, the blaze was completely vanquished. Only a sodden pile of ashes and debris at one end of the range of buildings showed blackly in the faint moonlight.

Gorini set two of the men on all-night watch in case any stray spark of life remained to burst out again, then we from the villa piled into the car and made for home.

When would he discover the loss of his horse? I wondered fearfully. But it was not to be tonight. Exhaustion sent us all to bed as soon as the villa had been securely locked, and on his part, Beppo could have no reason to suppose that anything was amiss behind the closed door of the stable. He, too, would tumble quickly into bed.

But the following day the storm broke.

Carlotta, Gorini, and I had assembled on time in the dining room, in spite of the disturbed night. Gorini was fuming because breakfast had not yet appeared and he wanted to get down to the buildings and see the extent of the damage by daylight, when there came an agitated knocking on the door, and in sidled Beppo looking positively scared.

I guessed at once what was coming.

"What now?" Gorini demanded testily. "Some new trouble?"

"Big trouble, signore," Beppo quavered. "Tarantula is gone from his stall."

I thought Gorini would strike him. He strode toward him, grasped him by both shoulders and shook him till his teeth rattled.

"What do you mean gone?" he bellowed.

"Missing signore," the unfortunate Beppo stuttered. "Stolen it seems, for saddle and bridle, they are gone also."

The roar that escaped his master was enough to make even the boldest quail. Spadoni, entering at that moment with a tray of coffee and hot rolls almost dropped the lot, and assuming that the outburst was aimed at him because breakfast was slightly late, began to make profuse apologies.

Gorini cut him short.

"What do you think this idiot Beppo has done?" he demanded. "Lost me the most expensive horse I ever had."

Spadoni set down the tray and stared in dismay.

"But surely the stable doors are kept locked?" Carlotta cut in.

Miserably Beppo shook his head. "There is no need for that as a rule, signorina. Before retiring for the night, I turn the dog loose at the back. He would tear to pieces any stranger who came snooping round. But last night all was confusion with the fire, and Signore Gorini took the dog with him to try and catch the culprit."

Stepping away from Beppo, Gorini thumped the table so hard that the china danced.

"*Mio, dio!*" he exclaimed, "now I see it all. There was but one rascal, and not content with burning down my buildings, he adds insult to injury by coming up here while the place was deserted and coolly making off with my mount. Small wonder I saw no trace of him."

Carlotta gave a smothered shriek. "Just imagine, Enrico. I was alone in the villa at the time. It turns my blood cold to think what might have happened had the villain decided on burglary first. Why, I could easily have been murdered in my bed. Surely the loss of even a good horse is small besides that possibility."

But Gorini ungraciously turned his back on her.

"He won't get away with it!" he swore. "I've got powerful friends. I'll set them looking for him. I've no time for breakfast this morning."

He poured himself a cup of coffee, gulped it down, grabbed a roll and stalked out, followed by Beppo and Spadoni.

"Remarkable how easily some people revert to type and shed every vestige of refinement on the least provocation," Carlotta said as she sat down at the table.

I followed suit and helped myself to coffee to steady my nerves. Gorini's threats had roused considerable apprehension on Angelo's behalf, and it was an effort not to show it.

An effort to calmly sit eating breakfast, too, when I wanted to be off spilling the news to Carlo. How would he take this new development?

Presently, on the plea of my hospital work, I made my escape and hurried off. But now that Carlo was up and moving around with the aid of a walking stick, it seemed that privacy was going

to be difficult to find. Nurse Ponti spent only a short time on
his rapidly healing wounds, then whisked me off to more urgent
cases in the main ward, without any chance to even pass Angelo's note.

Carlo, no doubt chafing as much as I was at this frustrating
state of affairs, stumped around the ward in as close pursuit
as he dared, so that when, behind the drawn screens round the
newest patient's bed Nurse Ponti sent me off to fetch clean
linen, I was able to pass the note with the urgent message. "I've
got to talk to you."

"I'll stick around and watch my chance," he murmured back,
as I hurried into the linen room.

It came at the end of the round when Nurse Ponti retired
to her cubbyhole to write up notes for the doctor. I left the
ward as usual but lingered in the passage, and sure enough
Carlo joined me a moment later.

"If anyone happens to come along, I'm practicing walking
farther afield," he said with a chuckle. "Now what's all the
mystery? Angelo says he is leaving the district for a safer hideout. A wise move no doubt. I'm all impatience to join him."

"He went last night," I murmured. "With a flourish that
set the villa astir. We have reason to believe that Gorini had
poor Francesca waylaid and murdered in the hills to stop her
talking, so Angelo determined to avenge her to the best of his
ability before he slipped away." Quickly I passed on the details
of our hectic night, ending with Angelo's daring exit on Gorini's
horse.

Carlo laughed. "Don't fret, he won't catch Angelo. He'll be
far away by now, and we've a network of trusty contacts to
aid us."

"That's some comfort," I said soberly, "especially when you,
too, leave the safety of the hospital to join him. I won't ask
where that is."

He shook his head. "You've been the most wonderful help.
I don't forget, ever. One day, when all this is over and Italy
has come to her senses, maybe I shall be able to do something

about it. Until then, we have a mighty struggle before us, I fear."

Somberly we stood, just looking at each other, then impulsively I took his face between my hands and kissed it, my lips roving softly over every firm feature and finally coming to rest against his. We stood locked together for a timeless moment, both conscious of the fact that it might well be our last chance to say farewell.

Chapter Twelve

How coolly beautiful was the patio that opened on to the gardens at the rear of the house. The vines rioting over the trellis-work above, already showing clusters of immature grapes, cast welcome deep shade on the marble mosaic floor below. A fountain played softly in the center while flowering shrubs of oleander, poinsettias, and hibiscus flaunted their scarlets and pinks in gay abandon in their ornate pots.

I sat in a basket chair, enjoying the luxury of idleness with the temperature eighty-five outside. Having no Angelo to sustain with food and news, my afternoons were now free. There was always Francesca's family of course, but since that last visit several days ago when her husband had confirmed that she was still missing, along with his fears that something bad had happened to her, I could not bring myself to return. Not yet. I knew too much and felt guilty in not telling him, but how could I do that, without exposing both Angelo and myself to the deadly wrath of Gorini and his gang? It would do nothing to bring back poor Francesca, or bring her murderers to justice. There was little justice in Calabria for the poor as Carlo and Angelo knew only too well. And they and the organization they stood for seemed the only ones to raise their hands in protest. How I wished I could do much more to help them.

My morning stints at the hospital were better than nothing, but how empty they would seem when Carlo was gone. And that could be any time now I realized bleakly. This morning he had seemed different. Keyed up as though with some dark secret. There had been no opportunity to speak to him alone.

Only the memory of yesterday's embrace, and the brooding glance he had cast my way.

There would still be David Crossley, I reflected with some comfort. My one friend and confidant in this sinister set-up. But prudence decreed I see little of him—scarcely enough to make life here at the villa, with a man I hated and feared, bearable.

Carlotta in no way helped. Mutual dislike existed between us, ever threatening to boil over. I could only despise her, while she oddly enough, seemed to be jealous of me and my presence at the villa.

How little cause she had for that, I thought with curling lip. But perhaps Enrico himself fed the ridiculous flame. At times he seemed to take a delight in taunting her with marked, and unwanted attentions toward me.

He startled me now by entering the patio so quietly that I was unaware of him until his two hands clamped themselves heavily on my shoulders.

"So! At last I have you to myself!" he said. "Now you can tell me all about that castle in Wales. Is it grander than this villa?"

"There's no comparing the two, they're so very different," I said, glad when he ceased to touch me and sprawled in a companion chair to mine. "Nantallon is gray and square and immensely strong, with feet-thick walls to stand the onslaughts it was once subjected to. The furniture is a complete contrast too. Centuries-old solid oak, some of it battered and worn. I'm sure you'd consider it quite ugly after the treasures here."

"That is a matter to be decided later. This cursed war has gripped everything by the throat and has us hamstrung. However, if Mussolini triumphs with Adolf Hitler, as he will, and Fascism reigns supreme, we shall then be free to travel again."

"Then you'll be far too busy restoring the trade and fortune of the citrus groves to think about castles in Wales," I said crisply. "As for me, I can't wait to leave Calabria behind and take up my life again there. I've no interests here."

Enrico leaned forward, grinning sardonically. "I'm not to be dismissed so lightly I warn you. I've yet to meet a woman able to stand against me, once I really set out to charm her."

A derisive laugh broke in on us. Carlotta stood there, two angry spots of color flaring in her cheeks.

"Your standards are falling, Enrico. Schoolgirls are scarcely to be classed as women!"

He turned, frowning. "I've told you before you don't own me. Now let us have no more nonsense. We're forced together by the exigencies of war. We must make the best of it and be good friends together. I intend to go and buy a new horse this afternoon, since Tarantula seems to have vanished into thin air. How would you both like to come for a drive?"

"Count me out," I said decisively. "I'm taking it easy today."

Carlotta smiled. "Very sensible, signorina. I shall be happy to accompany you, Enrico."

And yet, when they had gone, I could not rest. An uneasy feeling stole over me, tensing my whole body. Subconsciously I felt that something dramatic was brewing, but could not imagine what.

Had it something to do with Carlo, and the impression I had formed that he was about to leave the hospital and do something daring before he stole away to join Angelo. The vague hints he had previously let fall of having a score to settle with Gorini, haunted me. Recalling Angelo's narrow escape recently when he attempted something similar, I trembled for Carlo. Although he had made wonderful progress under the good hospital care, his leg was not yet up to normal performance. He needed a spell of convalescence in some safe place.

I did not see Carlotta and Gorini again until we met for dinner. They both seemed in good spirits. The latter had found a horse he approved of, while Carlotta flaunted a gold bracelet she had induced him to buy for her.

"Carlotta doesn't have the monopoly," Gorini said, glancing my way. "I have something for little Lisa too in my study. You shall have it in a moment."

While Spadoni cleared the pasta garnished with tomato sauce, and we waited for him to bring in the swordfish steaks,

Gorini rose to bring me the present I did not in the least want. I knew only too well that it was part of the process of wearing down my resistance. Carlotta might be all very well in his eyes for fun and games without the tie of marriage, but I presented a challenge he could not resist—a castle and estate in Britain, from which to spread his evil net farther afield.

Into my musing, from beyond the open dining-room door, came a startled shout. It was followed a few seconds later by two almost simultaneous gunshots.

Wide-eyed, Carlotta and I stared at each other, then sprang to our feet and raced out, across the marble entrance hall, and through the open door of Gorini's study.

A few paces inside he stood, blood pouring from his right wrist, a dropped gun at his feet. Opposite stood a masked figure, still pointing the gun that had caused the damage. Between was the huge desk forced open, which suggested robbery as the motive.

Carlotta screamed when she saw the blood and flung herself upon her lover in theatrical abandon, clinging to him for dear life. At the same moment, the masked man leaped from behind the desk and lunged through the doorway, brushing so close that his clothes touched mine.

"Let go, you fool!" Gorini roared, trying with his good left hand to push Carlotta aside. "Do you want the villain to escape?"

I scarcely heard him for the tingle of sheer excitement that shot through me at the momentary contact. That, and the noticeable limp of the escapee, convinced me that it was Carlo.

And in mortal danger of capture and slaughter, for from across the hall, I heard the enquiring shout of Spadoni running from the kitchen to investigate the shots.

In an agony of fear, I followed Carlo.

On seeing the masked intruder, Spadoni, now halfway across the hall and effectively cutting off escape through the front door, would undoubtedly have gone for him. But from within the study Carlotta called frantically, "Come quickly, Spadoni, your master is bleeding to death!"

He hesitated a moment, torn between two urges, and Carlo seized his chance, making for the remaining exit, the graceful marble staircase. With a bound he leaped to the lower steps, and up and away, still showing the limp to my hypersensitive gaze.

"You won't escape that way. I'll set the dog on your trail," Spadoni roared, before disappearing into the study to his master's aid.

On winged feet I raced up after Carlo, calling his name as I caught a glimpse of him in the first floor corridor, hesitating which way to go. Having no idea of the layout up here, it would be impossible for him to know in which direction escape lay.

Down from the hall raised voices indicated that they were on his track. There was only one recourse. I must hide him in my bedroom.

"They're coming. Trust me and follow me. It's your only chance!" I gasped, dashing to where a narrower staircase led up to less-opulent rooms, one of which was mine.

Without a word he followed, his only acknowledgment a fleeting touch on my elbow from behind.

We emerged on a less-imposing corridor. In the old days only servants would have occupied the rooms up here. Now there was merely the butler and cook, besides myself.

"The two servants are downstairs," I whispered. "If I open the end window they'll think you escaped that way. There's a flimsy fire escape leading down. You'd better not chance it yet though. You'd soon be caught with your lame leg when they turn out with the dog. My room seems safer until the hunt dies down."

I pushed open the door and closed it after us.

"They might well look in here," Carlo said, glancing round for a hiding place.

I nodded. "There's only one possibility. Under the bed with you. I shan't keep you there longer than absolutely necessary."

I raised the flowered valance that hung down to the floor and would give splendid cover. A little stiffly because of his leg, he dived beneath the high brass bed and lay full length on the dusty floor among the lumber.

"A little more protection in case anyone peers down here I think," I whispered, arranging various hat boxes and oddments that had been pushed away there out of sight, in front of him. Then I dropped the valance.

"Now I'm going to open that window and spin them a yarn," I hissed. "If anyone enters, don't move a muscle until I tell you it's safe."

I sped out, closing the door softly behind me. I could plainly hear voices on the floor below. At any moment they might come up here. There was no time to lose.

Swiftly I ran to the end of the corridor and with a struggle, unfastened the stiff casement window. Obviously it had not been used for years, but now could well save Carlo's life.

Peering out, I could dimly see the top of the narrow iron staircase that I had earlier noticed zigzagging down to ground level. Then leaving the window wide open, I hurried back down the corridor and descended the staircase to the main landing.

They were searching the main corridor. Gorini, a white linen napkin swathing his wrist, emerged from his bedroom closely followed by Carlotta. In the next room I could hear Spadoni lumbering around among the gilded furniture.

"Not a sign of the villain," the latter grunted, now appearing, "yet he made up the stairs, I saw him. You too, signorina. You were there!" Spadoni glared belligerently at me.

"Yes, where have you been in the meantime?" Carlotta demanded.

"Why, searching like you of course," I said glibly. "I followed him from the hall, and caught the tail end of him disappearing up the top flight. Although I'd have died of fright if he'd suddenly confronted me with that awful gun, I felt I ought to follow and see where he went. But when I reached the top floor, there was no sign of him. I couldn't pluck up courage to search the rooms alone and was just about to come down and get help when I felt a draught, and noticed that the window at the far end of the corridor was wide open. On going to investigate,

I saw an iron staircase leading down. Obviously, he's escaped that way."

"The fire escape! Damnation!" Gorini exploded. "Spadoni, go and collect the dog and search the grounds. You may have some luck. This cursed wrist puts me out of the chase. I'm bleeding like a stuck pig. Carlotta, run down and telephone Dr. Crossley to come and see to it. I don't like him, but any port in a storm. If it's serious, I'll have to go back to the hospital with him for further measures. At least that's close enough."

Carlotta turned away. Gorini did not follow as I'd hoped, but said, "While I'm waiting I'll take a look up there. I take nothing for granted. It could be a trick."

Surely he didn't suspect anything of the truth, I reflected in a panic as I followed him up the narrow flight.

He began a perfunctory search of the rooms. Fortunately for Carlo and me, he was hampered by his damaged right wrist and no doubt in considerable pain, for he merely flung open the wardrobe door, and then glanced under the bed when he started on the cluttered apartment of the Spadonis. By the time he reached my room, my heart thumped so loudly, that I felt sure he must hear it. However, he calmly flung open the wardrobe door, pulled aside the clothes, stared round the room then whisked up the valance to peer under the bed.

I felt I must die. Surely Carlo would be discovered now, in spite of the coverage of junk. The slightest movement, a sneeze or a cough caused by the dust, and we would both be in peril. But as Gorini bent to peer closer, a severe spasm of pain seemed to shoot through his wrist. With a frightful oath he straightened, clutching at the wound.

Oozing blood had now stained the napkin red. It looked pretty bad. Making a bold effort I grasped his good arm.

"You're in no fit state for this sort of thing," I said firmly. "And in any case, the doctor will be along any minute. Come down and have a drink while you wait. This is nothing but a waste of effort, since he obviously escaped through the window."

"No doubt you are right," he muttered through clenched

teeth. But he insisted on inspecting the open window, and then on my closing it firmly, before going down to the ground floor.

So far so good, I reflected. The situation for Carlo and me was still precarious, but with luck the worst could be over.

When Carlotta saw the deeply stained napkin, she declared she felt quite faint and flung herself down on a chaise longue in the drawing room. It was left to me to bring brandy for them both and then let Dr. Crossley in when he rang.

David Crossley warmly grasped my hand as he stepped into the hall.

"Glad to see you at least seem to have suffered no ill, signorina. I gather there's been a spot of bother with an intruder," he said.

I nodded. Did he know anything about the affair, or had Carlo taken French leave from the hospital? It was safer to act dumb.

"Signore Gorini surprised a masked burglar in his study," I explained. "They both used guns, but Enrico got the worst of it. He's wounded in the wrist. Please come this way, Doctor."

"So you have finally availed yourself of my help," he said cheerfully when face to face with his patient. "I'm glad to be of service to you, Signore Gorini. I called here often enough in Signore Moravia's days."

"So I believe." Gorini unwound the bloodsoaked napkin, exposing the wound.

Dr. Crossley probed delicately.

"Fortunately I don't think any bones are broken, but to be sure I should prefer an X-ray. In any case, you'll need a considerable number of stitches. You'll need to come back to the hospital with me."

Carlotta exclaimed in dismay.

"Oh, we shan't keep him too long," the doctor assured her. "And I promise to return him safely myself. After all, without the continued patronage of the Villa Caterina, our little hospital could not carry on. We are glad to do anything we can for a benefactor. Was the intruder caught, by the way?"

Gorini shrugged. "He certainly would have been, but for my

predicament. As it was, he escaped from an upstairs window. My man's out looking for him with a dog, so we may catch him yet."

"Well, I'll wrap something antiseptic round your wrist and we'll be off. The sooner it receives attention, the better. Now please bring me something that will act as a sling. It needs to be kept up," he added.

"A towel, I think," Gorini said, making for the cloakroom with Carlotta in his wake, and David Crossley and I were left face to face. His eyes burned with questions it was too dangerous to ask. How could I set his mind at rest?

"Swordfish have been at play this evening," I murmured quickly. "Now they lie in hiding."

"So. I suspected as much. They had better remain in hiding for the next hour or two, until the big bad spearers are safely back and in their beds," he whispered.

I nodded. With Gorini and Spadoni both at large, Carlo was certainly safer out of sight. Much better to go when they had retired.

There was no time to say more. Carlotta and Gorini were back, his wrist supported in a towel sling. The patient was led off by the doctor, and she and I were left to make what we could of the remainder of the evening.

"*Dio, mio!* What an evening this is turning out to be!" she exclaimed. "And only a few days after that shocking affair of the outbuildings fire and the theft of Enrico's horse. Someone certainly has a grudge against him. If this goes on, I shall be a nervous wreck and Naples, war or not, will be a haven of peace in comparison."

"Cheer up," I said drily. "Here comes Spadoni at least."

"And he drew a blank, by that sour expression. Well, perhaps he can now attend to his household duties. Do you realize, we've had no dinner, apart from the spaghetti course which I never touch for my figure's sake. See to it at once, Spadoni."

"I don't think I want any, not after all the excitement," I said, conscious of Carlo in his cramped hiding place. He would not dare leave it until I gave the word.

"Well why not take a tray up to your room," she suggested, perhaps glad to be free of me. "I shall wait up for Enrico and make sure he has some supper before I see him safely in bed."

I brightened. Nothing would suit me better. I could share the food with Carlo. I glowed at the thought of an intimate session, hidden away together.

"You must collect it yourself from the kitchen then," Spadoni growled. "I've only one pair of hands." He marched off, still muttering.

I followed him. The cook, all agog to hear the whole exciting story from firsthand, waved me toward the stove, while she and Spadoni sat at the huge center table, a bottle of wine between them, drinking and talking. Evidently Carlotta's needs took second place to Spadoni's creature comforts.

With their attention distracted, I slapped two substantial swordfish steaks onto a hot plate, added a dish of vegetables, some cutlery, a bottle of wine and Sicilian pastries. Then, with a quick *"Arrivederci"* I hurried off, before they noticed the quantity of food I carried.

With my bedroom door closed behind me, I set down the tray, raised the valance and said, "Now at last it's safe to come out. How cramped you must be!"

His healing leg had stiffened with the earlier strain put upon it. I had to help him up with both hands, and inevitably we found ourselves locked together.

"This is the second time you've saved my life, Lisa, *mia*," he murmured at last. "What an astonishing girl you are! What courage and resource!"

"That's merely because you bring out the best in everyone," I countered. "Now guess what we have for dinner? Swordfish! Isn't that appropriate."

He sniffed appreciatively. "My favorite dish. But how did you manage it, and what's going on below? I went through some damned unpleasant moments under that bed, certain I'd be discovered, especially when Gorini marched in and actually raised the valance."

"His wound got the better of him and saved you. I think he swallowed the suggestion that you'd escaped via the fire escape. At any rate, he sent Spadoni out with the dog, all to no purpose of course."

He looked a trifle wary.

"Where are they all now? What's to prevent them coming up here again and hearing our voices?"

"Gorini's gone off to hospital for attention, Carlotta is impatiently awaiting his return to fuss over him. Neither will trouble to climb up here again tonight, I'm certain. As for the butler and cook, they're busy in the kitchen. They won't be finished for ages yet, as they'll need to stay on duty until their master returns and has been fed. So that gives you plenty of time to enjoy your food in comfort. What are your plans after that? Are you returning to the hospital?"

He nodded. "Just for tonight. At daybreak I'll be off. They'll transport me in an ambulance as a stretcher case, the way they often smuggle rebels out and in. It's surprising what a splendid disguise a roll of bandage about the head and face can achieve."

I smiled. "Then the best time for you to slip away from here via the fire escape is after Gorini gets back and before the Spadonis come up here to bed. We couldn't risk any noise after that."

"Shall you hear him come in at this height?"

"Spadoni brought the dog indoors with him, so he's certain to bark, no matter who comes in. You know, that's another lucky break for you, Carlo. Normally, the dog roams the gardens at night. It could have made things hazardous for you climbing down to the ground. Now let's eat."

I sat on the bed, he took the single chair, with the tray between us on a rickety bamboo table.

"Do you mind us both using the same plate?" I asked. "I didn't dare bring two in case they suspected something when I took it down to wash up. I was lucky to get away with two helpings of food."

His eyes caressed me. "I would eat from your hand if necessary, Lisa, *mia*."

"That won't be necessary. I did chance two forks. Take your pick of the vegetables. The beans look delicious."

How merry was the following half hour. As merry as a stolen dormitory feast in days gone by. But infinitely more tender and precious, because of the parting that must come after and the growing uncertainty of where he would be, what dangers he would face, and when, if ever, we would meet again.

"By the way," I said as he bit into the last pastry, "what made you take the risk of breaking into Gorini's study while you knew he would be at dinner? The hope of funds for the cause, I suppose. Did you find anything to make it worthwhile?"

He nodded. "A substantial sum, but I had even better luck than that. The object I hoped might be there was indeed tucked away in a drawer of his desk. Since he stole it from my father in the first place, I had no qualms about pocketing it. I'll show it to you."

He took out the most exquisite wristwatch I had ever seen. Its dainty gold bracelet and dial frame were studded with what could only have been genuine diamonds, their glitter unmistakable.

"It must be worth a small fortune," I gasped.

"Undoubtedly, but the sentimental value is even greater to me, since it belonged to my dead mother."

"No wonder you hate Gorini."

His sensitive lips compressed with bitterness. "That's merely the half of it, Lisa *mia*. Enrico Gorini killed my father as surely as though he'd stabbed him through the heart, by denouncing him to the Fascists as a Royalist traitor, plotting to kill high-ranking leaders. The charges were mostly false, his trial was a mockery, and he was executed by firing squad with indecent haste. All his property was confiscated, leaving me with nothing. Gorini, of course, got his hands on the watch and other small valuables before other Fascist vultures could close in. I swore vengeance then that one day Gorini would pay with his life for his crimes."

I said soberly, "You've had provocation enough, heaven knows. I wonder you managed to confine yourself to merely wounding him this evening, instead of going the whole way. It would have settled my score with him too."

"Fortune was with him tonight, and against me. When Gorini entered the study and saw me at the desk, he grabbed his gun from an open drawer. I pulled out my own. We fired almost simultaneously. I had to jerk sideways to escape his bullet, which put my own aim off true. My fire merely caught his raised hand and wrist, putting it out of action. That was my perfect opportunity to kill him, yet oddly I couldn't do it because he was defenseless. I suppose that makes me sound pretty feeble."

"No, I'd have felt the same. And then Carlotta and I appeared and your chance was gone."

He nodded. "It will come again, I'll see to that. In the meantime, will you do something for me?"

"Certainly."

He placed the watch in my hand. "Keep this safe for me as a token of my regard. If fate decrees we never meet again, it is yours, to do with as you please."

Tears sprang to my eyes. I could not say a word.

"With no settled home and in the hazardous situations in which I land myself, I can't take it with me. It would be lost or stolen," he said. "You must hide it under lock and key though. It would go badly with you if Gorini ever discovered you had it in your possession."

"I know. But rest assured, Carlo, I'll keep it safe and pray that the time won't be too long before you are able to reclaim it." Forcing a laugh, I added, "What on earth is he going to say when he searches his desk and finds it missing?"

Carlo smiled grimly. "If he blows his top enough, he might go off in a stroke!"

There came the faint barking of a dog down in the hall.

"He's back," I whispered. "Now is your best chance to get safely away while they are all occupied. Come."

We crept along the corridor. Carlo thrust open the window, climbed through on to the top of the fire escape and turned, his face level with mine.

There was so much to say, and no further time to say it. Our faces were pale in the moonlight as we looked at each other for a long moment. "God be with you," I whispered, and then he began his careful descent.

I watched the top of his lustrous black head recede until he reached the ground. He glanced up, raised his hand in silent farewell, then slipped away into the dark and hostile night.

Chapter Thirteen

Enrico's wrath exploded the following morning, when he came in to breakfast after going through his desk.

"That damned bandit has made off not only with a considerable sum of money, but with a valuable watch besides!" he stormed. "Obviously part of the same gang of miscreants who stole my horse and set fire to the plantation buildings. Some of them must be still lurking around, and I propose to get them before they strike again."

"But didn't your men make a search after the last outrage," I said mildly, "and find nothing?"

He shrugged his great shoulders. "I wouldn't say they found nothing. In fact, they made one valuable elimination. Unfortunately, not one of this audacious gang."

So there it was, I reflected with cold fury. A tacit admittance of Francesca's murder, although he would never dream I knew anything of that affair. What a cold-blooded monster he was, with three deaths on his conscience that I knew of, and no doubt others besides. Anything that Carlo could do to avenge his father, dear Margaret, and poor Francesca, would be only common justice. It was a pity last night's bullet had not reached a more fatal target.

To mask my feelings I asked how his hand and wrist were.

"Stiff and sore, but no bones broken. That doctor knows his job, I'll say that for him, but it's time I had some return for the money this estate has poured into the hospital. At all events, the wrist's not bad enough to stop me riding, especially as I want to try out my new horse."

Carlotta glanced at the neat bandage. "You'd be better off

staying here and resting it," she said petulantly. "You know I don't ride, and I don't propose to sit twiddling my thumbs alone here most days. That, coupled with the hazards of bandits around here, would tip the scales in favor of a return to Naples."

He smiled. "You're a free agent, Carlotta, *mia*. Why do you suppose I've never succumbed to your blandishments hopelessly enough to marry you, if not because I refuse to be tied down by any woman. The one I marry must dance to my tune. You would never do that."

Characteristic angry spots of color flared in her cheeks.

"I've more spirit, perhaps providentially, since your tune is apt to turn out a macabre dance, Enrico, *mio*."

He said furiously, "Watch your tongue, you she-cat. You may do as you please, but I mean to try out my new horse and see if I can flush out any of that gang at the same time. Since my right hand is not up to shooting, I'll take someone with me guaranteed not to bungle if we spot anyone. You, too, shall go, Lisa, *mia*. You ride well enough to comb the rough hill country and should be an asset with your sharp eyes."

"But they'll be expecting me at the hospital," I protested.

"Since you don't get paid, you are under no obligation. Any resident of the Villa Caterina is looked on with respect by the hospital's head, who is greatly in our debt. Phone up Dr. Crossley to say you will not be in today."

Mutiny struggled within me. I wanted to hear from Dr. Crossley how Carlo had fared after his escape from here. But it didn't matter enough to cause a row and possibly rouse Gorini's suspicions. Unless unforeseen bad luck had prevailed, Carlo should be well away from the hospital by now, so I would have few qualms in joining in a search for rebels. Now that both Angelo and Carlo were safely out of the vicinity, I reflected, Gorini would draw a blank.

"As you wish," I said. A ride in the hills would be delightful on such a morning, even with distasteful companions.

I went into Enrico's study to use the phone, ringing through to David Crossley's office. Could I be overheard at this end?

I wondered, conscious of the open study door. Caution was certainly necessary.

"Afraid I shan't be coming in this morning," I explained. "Not from choice, you understand, but force of circumstances. One thing I'd like to know. What of Swordfish?"

"On his way." He sounded as cautious as I, but added as though anxious about me, "Everything all right at your end?"

I caught the sound of movement in the doorway. Enrico had either been listening just outside or was coming in to snoop.

"Yes," I said hastily. "Must ring off now. I'm going riding. Good-bye."

Enrico was frowning when he faced me across the desk.

"Who or what is 'Swordfish'?" he demanded.

A tremor shot through me. Think fast, Lisa my girl, if you're to fool him. Think fast.

"Swordfish? Why, it's the nickname of an old fisherman now retired. He was brought in yesterday with a perforated appendix needing immediate operation. It was touch and go, so I wanted to know if he'll make it, and was glad to hear he will." My facile invention surprised even myself.

Enrico looked unconvinced. "Seems to me I've heard that expression before in connection with those resistance fighters," he growled.

I managed a laugh. "You're absolutely obsessed with the resistance rebels! Small wonder really, after their recent unwelcome attentions. But you must know what a common word swordfish is around here, it being a local delicacy and the Straits of Messina so famous for the distinctive sword-fishing boats."

"Maybe. Well, let's be off before it grows too hot for comfort."

A pair of slacks and a cool shirt were the only riding habit necessary or comfortable in this climate. Evidently they were becoming, too, for Enrico stared appraisingly at me as we set off.

"Carlotta flatters herself on her attractions," he said, "but you make her look like an overblown peony."

He could keep his flattery as far as I was concerned. Not only was it distasteful, but in a way frightening. It pointed so clearly to his designs on me and my Welsh estate.

I put on a spurt and forged ahead.

"Hang on," he called as I made for the rugged hills. "I'm enlisting help from the castle. Shan't be more than a few minutes."

He turned in at the rusting iron gates and was swallowed up in the gaping hole that had once been an impressive portal.

I paused, staring up at the broken pile, feeling no urge to follow him. Since my first venture the place had repelled me. Now that I knew it was the meeting place of the local Mafia I feared it even more, and hoped that Carlo and Angelo would never be driven again to taking shelter in the cave so close to this spider's lair.

Enrico soon reappeared, a horseman in tow. Not the old man I had once seen in the castle, but a burly ruffian, dark-skinned and unkempt, who looked capable of betraying his own mother.

He turned a lowering glance on me and passed some remark in Italian to Enrico as they made off into the hills, I following.

"What does he say?" I called. "If he has any objections to my company, I'm willing enough to go off on my own."

Enrico glanced round. "Stay where you are. As a matter of fact, he says he's seen you in the hills before. Once he tried to follow you, but you disappeared. What's the fascination of this wilderness for you? Most young girls would be afraid to venture here alone."

My mouth went dry. "Why, I love hills and mountains as all Welsh people do," I protested in a voice that sounded too shrill. "They're perfect for horse riding."

"You were on foot, not riding. Where did you disappear to?"

I could not answer. Presently Enrico's companion turned off down a narrower track into the ravine, that petered out among the great boulders and rocks where I had once eaten my picnic lunch and then heard the groans of Carlo, coming faintly from the cave.

"I did have a picnic here once. My first day in Almina," I

said then as innocently as I could. "Afterward I explored a bit, but was afraid to go far for fear of getting lost. Since then, I've both walked and ridden around occasionally in an afternoon."

"And seen no one? Heard nothing?"

"Not surprisingly, no. If any outlaw lurked around, as you seem to imagine, he'd take care to keep well hidden and make no sound during the day at least. That makes sense doesn't it?"

He only grunted. His companion spoke again, dismounted, tethered his horse and began to wander in and out among the maze-like rocks. Enrico followed suit, and I, morbidly anxious now, trailed after.

At first they moved in any direction save that of the cave, but presently, to my consternation, they began to drift closer to it. Alberto, as the stranger was named, led the way, moving slowly inch by inch, his eyes boring like gimlets into the rough ground and craggy rocks on either hand.

Inevitably, at last he reached the section just outside the cave where Angelo had lit his fire. A quick glance showed me that the curtain creepers hung naturally in place, effectively concealing the cramped entrance, but Alberto had stopped dead, staring more intently than ever at the ground for any evidence of human interference with nature.

The debris of coarse grass and undergrowth strewn around by Angelo some days earlier in an effort to hide the traces of a fire, now gave him away. Withered and browned by the heat, they contrasted sharply enough with the bare stony tracks about us to arouse Alberto's suspicions. He bent and began to scrabble among them with his horny hands, laying bare a few blackened fragments of twigs and pockets of gray ash.

"A fire was lit here," he growled, straightening.

"When?" Enrico's expression took on that of a tiger on the scent.

"A few days past I think." Alberto began to circle the small clearing, touching, listening, inspecting.

Enrico did the same, moving the opposite way, and he it was

who found the entrance to the cave when he carelessly pulled aside the creeper.

"*Dio, mio!* Here is the villain's hideout!" he exclaimed, stooping and thrusting his powerful frame inside.

Alberto followed. I, in a cold sweat in spite of the heat, trailed after.

The twilight revealed nothing of human habitation. Angelo's few possessions had gone easily into a rucksack which had been slung on his back that stirring night he had made off.

But Enrico was not satisfied.

"What's wanted is more light," he said. "Outside with you, Lisa, and raise that damned creeper."

I complied. Not to co-operate would only have aroused suspicion against me. Besides, what was there to find?

Only a crumpled bit of paper, screwed into a ball, tossed into a corner and overlooked on Angelo's departure. But for Enrico's insistence on more light it would never have been discovered now. As it was, Alberto's gimlet eyes ferreted it out, and with a grunt of triumph he passed it to his leader.

Enrico carefully unfolded it to reveal a foot square of soft white paper. With a dreadful sinking feeling I realized that it was the paper napkin I had wrapped round the bread that first day I had discovered the cave and its secret.

The two men thrust their way into the open, the better to examine their find. Immediately Enrico let out an astonished oath, for there quite clearly in blue across one corner, were the letters A.H.

"Almina Hospital!" he ground out. "Those initials head their notepaper and everything!"

Alberto stared stupidly. "Maybe the villains raid the hospital for food like they raid the villa," he put forward at last.

Enrico shrugged. "Maybe. But I smell a rat. Someone at the hospital could be on the side of the rebels. In liaison with them. Helping them in any way possible when any of them happened to be in the vicinity. I've heard one or two vague rumors. By heaven if they turn out to be true . . . !"

I felt like death. It would be a dreadful thing if he were able to pin anything definite on David Crossley and his secret band. In addition to withdrawing all funds and so crippling the hospital financially, so powerful a man as Enrico could denounce them as a nest of traitors against the state, with either death or imprisonment as punishment.

At any cost this must be avoided.

"Have you ever seen any of the hospital staff snooping around on the hills?" Enrico asked his follower.

Alberto shook his head. "Only her." He pointed an accusing finger at me.

Enrico looked sharply at me as though a thought had just struck him. "By heaven," he said softly, "and you work at the hospital, don't you my little innocent? You wouldn't, by any chance, have been playing Florence Nightingale or Lady Bountiful to a nest of tarantulas, would you?"

I stared, playing for time, thinking with the speed of desperation. In the face of this concrete evidence of hospital involvement, Enrico would move heaven and earth to track down the truth. It was either the hospital or me. If I accepted full responsibility, it might deflect his attention from David Crossley and his loyal aides, and they and their vital work would be saved. And if I played the innocent convincingly enough, I might even save myself as well.

"Come on, talk!" he demanded. "Where do you fit into this business? You'd better tell me everything before I lose patience."

"Oh, don't sound so cross as though I'd committed a crime," I protested with as much wide-eyed innocence as I could muster. "All I did was to give a little food to two ragged, starving schoolboys."

"Schoolboys! There are some damned young rebels about, I dare say, but they've come to something if they're recruiting schoolboys."

"Well, they didn't look any older," I said earnestly, "and how was I to know they were rebels—if they really were. They could hardly speak a word of English, and you know how hopeless I am with Italian."

"How did you first come across them?"

"I was out in the hills and caught the scent of wood smoke," I improvised, determined to keep my story as far from the truth as possible. "I hunted around and found these two youngsters trying to roast a fish they had caught in the river. They looked pretty miserable, so unkempt and hungry that I felt sorry for them, thinking they'd perhaps run away from some cruel stepfather or something. I was working at the hospital by then, so the following morning I collected some rolls left over from breakfast and brought them up here, wrapped in that paper. They made short work of them."

"And did you repeat the performance?"

I shook my head. "I went shopping in town the following day. I meant to help them again, but that evening the outbuildings were set alight and your horse stolen. I felt terribly upset and slightly guilty, wondering if it could have been those two youths."

"Yet you never breathed a word to me," he said drily.

"I was too scared. You can be pretty daunting at times, you know. Besides, I felt sure that if they *were* at the bottom of it, they'd soon be caught, riding your distinctive horse. It's odd how it just seemed to vanish."

"Odder still to have a second outrage perpetrated on me a few days later, don't you think? That masked gunman was no schoolboy at least."

I shrugged. "Now you've taken on the role of Master of the Villa Caterina, and with the country at war, you can expect to be a target for bandits. Me, I'm darned glad I've nothing to lose or steal. Not in this country anyway."

He almost smiled then, but it was a sour attempt. Impossible to tell whether he believed me or not. We continued ranging the hills for another hour, then he gave up and headed back to the villa, complaining that his new horse had a vicious temper, and was reluctant to obey him.

"I'll teach him better manners before he's much older," Enrico said as we dismounted at the stables. "Right now I need a stiff drink."

He gave the animal a mean cut with his riding crop before stalking off, leaving Beppo to cope with the now incensed beast.

"He won't get the best out of the creature with that treatment," I said indignantly as I led my mare to her stall, the stable lad following with Guiseppi.

Beppo tried to soothe the animal as he unharnessed him, but Guiseppi was by now thoroughly rattled. At a gasp of pain from Beppo, I swung round to see him clutching his left upper arm, bared by rolled up sleeves, where the nervous beast had turned on him in a panic and inflicted a nip.

"How very unfair for you to reap the consequences of Signore Gorini's mismanagement," I said, moving to the unfortunate lad's side. "He called the horse ill-tempered, but he's just as bad. Have you anything I can use for a bandage? He's given you a nasty nip and it's starting to bleed."

Beppo opened a cupboard door and pulled out a shirt, ragged beyond wear, but bleached white by the sun. I tore off a strip and glanced among the bottles and boxes for an antiseptic.

They were mostly horse remedies, but amongst them I found some disinfectant. With this I liberally doused his already discoloring wound, then wound the bandage gently but firmly round.

"You are kind," he said wonderingly.

After a long pause, I said, "You know, Signore Moravia was my father. And the lady who came out for his funeral and then married Signore Gorini was my sister. Did you see much of her?"

His face became doleful. "Not much. She was kind to me, like you, but so soon she died."

There was a curious expression on his face, fear struggling with some other emotion. At last he blurted out, "If you stay here, maybe you die too."

Ghostly hands seemed to touch my spine, bringing a quick shiver.

"If you can tell me anything at all about Signora Margaret, I should be most grateful," I said quietly. "I never believed her death to be natural, so I came here to find out."

Beppo nodded, glancing uneasily round as though he feared eavesdroppers.

"They said it was cholera killed Signora Margaret," he murmured hoarsely, "but she sick before that." He rubbed his stomach, rolling his eyes as though in great pain, then bent over in a mock copy of retching.

"Just as I suspected," I murmured. "Have you any idea what caused it, Beppo?"

He turned to the cupboard, and rummaged among the muddle of bottles and boxes until he found a green-glass bottle labeled "Antimony. Poison."

"Lots of rats around the stables," he explained. "I just put this on food and leave it beside their holes. It kills them."

"But what has this to do with Margaret?"

He lowered his voice still further until it was a mere whisper. "When the master bring his new wife here, he take away my bottle. I order a new one. Master say rats in the patio, but no rats there. I know."

My mouth went dry. The implication was clear.

"Can you put a few grains of it into something smaller?" I asked when I could speak. "I'd like to get an expert's opinion on it."

I was thinking of the old dispenser at the hospital. He would know about this noxious stuff and its effects.

Beppo rummaged again until he found an empty phial, then carefully transferred a little of the poison to it.

"You will not let Signore Gorini see it?" he said fearfully as he passed it to me. "You will not tell him anything of this?"

I shook my head.

I thrust the phial into the pocket of my slacks, then left to wash and change for lunch.

Here, almost certainly, I reflected sadly, was the cause of Margaret's untimely death. The cholera epidemic had merely been a fortuitous cover-up, from Gorini's point of view, averting any suspicion that might otherwise have fallen on him.

As I reached the villa, my loathing of him had grown to an even greater depth. No fate was too bad for such a monster.

Chapter Fourteen

I arrived early at the hospital the following morning, went round to the back, and waited until the dispenser was alone. Then I slipped into the small building and produced my phial.

"This was taken from a bottle marked 'Antimony,'" I said. "What can you tell me about it, and the effects if administered to human beings?"

The old man shook out a few grains, examined them through his steel-rimmed spectacles, then said, "This is certainly antimony, signorina. Not the sort of thing for you to play about with, or even have in your possession. A possible killer, in fact."

I nodded. "I understand it has been used to control rats, but what would be the effect on the human system, Signore Bonetti?"

He pursed his lips. "Well, it is certainly less lethal than some poisons. Slower working unless administered in large doses. If taken in small amounts, it would cause vomiting and stomach cramps, along with general debility and wasting away, similar to a number of diseases. An increased dose could cause death, of course, especially on a constitution already weakened."

My hands clenched at my sides. "In other words, very similar to the symptoms of cholera. Would you say an antimony poisoning could be passed off as a cholera death?"

"Quite easily, I should think, without a close investigation, especially if there happened to be an epidemic around at the time."

"Thank you very much, Signore Bonetti."

He placed his hand on my shoulder as I turned to go.

"I will not probe, signorina. Our movement survives on

secrecy and discretion above all things. All I ask is that you take the greatest care. Living at the villa as you are forced to do is like being enmeshed in a spider's web. At any moment the spider may dart."

"I know," I said soberly. "I'll certainly take care."

Later in the morning I managed to snatch a few words in private with David Crossley. He was not in the least surprised at my revelation, as he admitted that he had always entertained doubts regarding my half sister's death, but not having been called in on the case, could do nothing. He, too, expressed fears for my safety and advised care. His concern was deep and touching.

"Don't fret," I said with assumed confidence. "Gorini's quite interested in Nantallon Castle. I'm probably safe so long as he hopes to wear down my resistance and marry me for the sake of it. If ever that happened, I wouldn't bet on a long life!"

"And I wouldn't bet on *anything* where he is concerned," the doctor said grimly. "If he considered you a threat, or that you were working against him, you'd be just another fly to be eliminated."

I made an effort to change the subject by asking about Carlo.

"The best thing you can do, my dear Lisa, is to forget he even exists. His chosen path is too hazardous to permit thoughts of anything else, and that goes for me too. The pleasures most men take for granted are lost to us for the time being. If only it were otherwise . . ." He broke off, but his expression finished the sentence more eloquently than any words.

David Crossley was in love with me.

To cover my confusion I blurted out the first thing that came into my mind, "At least we can be glad that both Angelo and Carlo are far away from this danger spot." Recalling yesterday's incident at the cave, I meant it with all my heart.

"Glad indeed. Possibly in Naples, if that's any comfort."

"A big city."

"An ideal one in which to hide, to make plans and carry out attacks on the enemy."

On the way to the secret ward, I debated whether or not

to mention yesterday's jolting incident, but decided against worrying him needlessly since Gorini had apparently accepted my explanation. Nor had he forbidden me to go anymore to the hospital.

Carlotta left the villa soon after, to practice for the reopening of the San Carlo Opera House, for Naples had suffered little damage to date. In one respect I regretted her departure. It left me alone with Gorini, except for the servants, and I was beginning to fear him.

"I've decided on a trip to Naples myself," Enrico Gorini declared one morning at breakfast. "The San Carlo is opening on Thursday with *La Bohème*. Carlotta plays Mimi, her favorite role. She'll be highly offended if I don't turn up to see her."

"You, maybe. My absence will cause no regrets. You'll both be happier without me."

He shrugged. "Why must you always assume that Carlotta means more to me than any other woman? You ought to know different by now."

He certainly lost no opportunity to press his unwelcome attentions on me. Now that Carlotta was no longer here it was becoming quite embarrassing. At other times, with a prickling of the skin, I could sense him watching me, weighing up how much I knew against him, whether my work at the hospital involved more than caring for genuine patients, and on whose side I would be if it came to a showdown.

I remembered that Carlo might be in Naples. How I ached to see him, hear his tolerant, tender laughter, feel his mouth warm against my own. Suddenly I wanted to go to Naples more than anything. But I must be careful not to show it too clearly.

"Well, if you'd really like to have me along, it would be fun," I conceded. "At least there'll be some decent shops. What heaven it will be to buy a few things I really need, even if it does swallow up my few remaining lire. I'm beginning to feel like a street urchin, with nothing but what I brought in my case."

"You'll have carte blanche! I'll foot the bill," he said with a burst of generosity. "I realize your difficulties. It must be gall-

ing after your affluent life in Wales, having only the few things
you brought out with you.

"This is Tuesday. We'll go by train tomorrow morning," he
decreed. "You can finish with the hospital for good. Such work
is beneath you."

At the moment I did not dare to argue. On my return I
would face that issue, and make a stand if I decided it was safe
to do so. The last thing I wanted was to arouse Gorini's suspicions again regarding David and his secret work.

In anticipation of the slow, tedious journey through the hills,
Enrico had booked the best compartment he could on the
attenuated steam train that wound its tortuous way to the coast
once a day. While he settled himself in with luggage and reading matter, I amused myself by watching the peasants crowd
into the uncomfortable third-class carriages, their unwieldy bun-
dles of cardboard boxes tied with string piled about them. They
chattered away like parrots in their shrill Italian voices, no
doubt on their way to market, to buy or sell in other sleepy
little white and red towns that dotted the hillsides and valleys.

Above the station and town, the ruined castle frowned down
like some brooding giant on its now parched hillside. As always,
now that I knew what dark deeds were planned there, it brought
a swift surge of fear. It required an effort, when the whistle
blew, to climb in beside Enrico for the protracted journey.

It would have been a day of unbearable tension but for the
many stops, each one an opportunity to hop out onto the bak-
ing concrete platforms, stretch one's limbs, and refresh hands
and face at the water taps invariably to be found there. Food
and drink was no problem with a well-packed picnic basket, but
I had little appetite, being too tense at having to parry Enrico's
searching questions regarding the estate in Wales, my work at
the hospital, and similar supercharged topics.

But eventually we reached the great, sprawling city of Naples,
with its contrasts of beauty and squalor, in the shadow of
mighty Vesuvius that had boiled into fury in A.D. 79 and destroyed the neighboring city of Pompeii.

"You can shop tomorrow," Enrico said as we were whisked

away in a taxi to our hotel. "You'll need something dressy for a first night at the San Carlo. Perhaps Carlotta will advise you, if she happens to be in a good mood."

"I want no advice," I said tartly. "I'm not still in the school-room you know."

The heat of late summer lay heavily on the city as we stepped from the taxi. It came fiercely back from the pavement like a breath from a furnace. Even the fountain in the center of the piazza seemed to have expired of ennui, with merely a trickle spouting from the mouths of the dolphins.

Enrico stalked into the hotel, leaving me to follow and a liveried commissionaire to bring in our luggage.

"I shall be going out to dinner," he said as we checked in at the desk. "You had better have something sent up to your room. I'll order it now."

So he was meeting Carlotta or else some of his Mafia cronies. But after such a tiring day, I was not averse to turning in early.

How different it would have been had Carlo and I been in touch . . . he would somehow have contrived to meet me. The longing to see him was a torment that stayed with me all night.

But the next day, inevitably my spirits rose as I stared from my window at the busy piazza. Small boys and girls, almost indistinguishable in their blue smocks and white bows, ran laughing and chattering past the fountain on their way to school. Brown-robed friars, heads bent, hands clasped in their sleeves, strolled sedately toward the ornate church in the far corner. Pavement cafés already had customers for coffee, while sober, black-clad matrons passed laden from the early market.

Enrico, probably due to a late night session with Carlotta, was not so dewy fresh at breakfast.

"You must manage your shopping on your own I fear," he said. "Carlotta declares she must rest this morning to be fresh for the evening. As for me, I've things to do, people to see. Everything closes for the siesta in the early afternoons, of course, so it's now or never."

"That's how I prefer it," I said. "If you'll call me a taxi and direct it to the best department store I'll do well enough. No doubt some of the assistants will have a smattering of English."

"Of course." He passed across a purse. "Enough lire there for all you need, so spend what you please."

It went against the grain to take money from him, even though he had artfully annexed my rightful inheritance. My reluctance showed in my stilted thanks.

"I'll expect repayment, in one way or another, later," he said sardonically. "I'm not philanthropic enough to give without return."

But for my plight I should have flung it back in his arrogant face. But I was desperately in need of clothing replenishment, from top to toe, apart from the more frivolous extravagances necessary for a night at the opera. So I drained my coffee cup while he imperiously gave orders to the waiter and in a short time the man returned to say my taxi was at the door.

"I'll probably see you at lunch," Enrico said as I rose. "Mind what you get up to. There are crooks in plenty in Napoli."

And none more crooked than he, I reflected, padding across the carpeted expanse of the foyer and out into the comparative coolness of the morning air.

It was an amusing morning, wandering through the various departments of the great store and trying to make myself understood. The assistants were cheerful and obliging however, and eventually I had everything I needed, including a smart dress and shoes for the evening.

No doubt the store, if requested, would have sent everything to the hotel, but having spent so many lire, I could not bear to be parted from my pretty things. So laden with packages, I made my way out of the imposing entrance and stood blinking in the strong sunlight, looking for a taxi.

At the moment there seemed none about, though the street was packed with smart Italian cars, crawling bumper to bumper. Evidently the war had not yet affected the petrol allocation of the rich. The pavement, too, was crowded with less affluent shoppers, these looking more prosperous than the peasants of Almina.

And then, such an emotional shock flashed through me that

I almost dropped my load. For there, where a side street intersected this main thoroughfare, dodging across the road among several other pedestrians went Carlo.

I caught only a glimpse of him as he weaved his way between the crawling cars, but how could I not recognize a face etched so indelibly on my mind?

Frantic to contact him I started forward, calling his name aloud. But it was hopeless. An importuning street seller of lottery tickets caught at my arm, urging me to buy. Two of my packages fell from my grasp, and when I had picked them up again there was no sign of the tall arresting form.

To try to follow was useless. I knew which side street had swallowed him up, but even if I had managed the hazardous crossing of the road it would have been all in vain. He would have vanished again. A horse-drawn *carrozza* now materialized and paused beside me.

At the driver's hopeful *"Carrozza, signorina?"* I nodded, dumped my parcels inside and climbed in after them, giving him the name of my hotel.

I felt terrible. If I wandered the streets of Naples for weeks I might never again catch a glimpse of him. And, of course, that was impossible, because in a day or two I should be on my way back to Almina, without his ever knowing of that brief, tantalizing sighting.

The slow, horse-drawn drive that could have been so vividly interesting was wasted on me. I paid little attention to the cavernous side streets festooned with washing, the splendid baroque architecture, the dark, vivacious citizens. I was too sunk in my own frustration.

It was an effort to answer Enrico's questions regarding my shopping expedition with any animation. My emotional turmoil was still too great. I was glad when lunch was over and I could retire to my room, darkened behind closed shutters, to rest on my bed until the fierce heat of early afternoon passed. But though physically at rest, my mind seethed. Tomorrow morning, I decided, if Enrico left me alone, I should again take a taxi as far as the department store, and then follow the trail down that side street, hoping and praying that by some miracle I would again see him, this time close enough to contact.

And then it was time to dress for the opera. I had chosen an appealing gown in misty blue chiffon, that brought out the blueness of my eyes. The silver trim matched my silver sandals, and even in my present mood of frustration I had to admit that never had I looked so attractive.

If only Carlo had been my escort, or dear David Crossley.

Enrico stared when he saw me.

"So our little Cinderella is transformed into the princess," he said. "How very charming, my dear. Any man would be proud to partner you. You must certainly join the celebration party afterward, and later I shall contrive to have you to myself."

I shivered in distaste, already thinking up an excuse to avoid his unwelcome attentions.

San Carlo Opera House looked surprisingly drab from the outside, with even the fountain silent. Inside was a different story. All baroque splendor of stucco and gold, with the auditorium rising tier upon tier above the well of the stalls.

Carlotta had secured a stage box for Enrico. I felt very self-conscious sitting there in full view of the audience crowding into their seats. The vast sea of faces below, opposite, and lining the sides, all seemed to be staring up at us in my heightened imagination. Merely illusion, of course, although we must have made a striking couple, he so hugely arresting in his evening dress, I so appealingly small.

When the lights dimmed and Puccini's plaintive music filled the air with magic, excitement gripped me. My first opera, yet shared with my greatest enemy. Could anything be more ironic.

Carlotta made an arresting Mimi, I had to acknowledge. Her voice was superb, full of pathos and expression. As the plaintive notes of the first act died away and the lights went up, Enrico rose.

"Must look in and congratulate Carlotta in her dressing room. She'll be expecting me," he said as he hurried off.

Alone, I felt more exposed to public gaze than ever. Carried away by the pathos of the opera, my cheeks were flushed and damp with stray tears. I needed the ladies' powder room to recuperate, and to this end I made my way toward it.

Afterward, able to face the world again but not wanting to return to the empty stage box, I wandered down the stairs, past the bar around which clustered a milling crowd, and into the auditorium, to see what the theater looked like from this angle.

It was magnificent. How much self-confidence Carlotta must have to stand up on that great stage, the target of every eye, and sing for her supper. But, of course, she had looks, voice, and poise in plenty, and well she knew it.

The audience, jostling past me back to their seats, reminded me that the interval was almost over and the next act about to start. Glancing up at the stage box, I noticed that Enrico had returned, and it was high time I did the same.

Easier said than done, with so many stragglers all bent on gaining their seats. And then the main lights dimmed, leaving only small side lights to illuminate the place, and it became more difficult than ever.

I reached the entrance of the auditorium. Now there was only the foyer and the stairs to negotiate. Behind me the orchestra began to tune up, and then, at the staccato sound of a pistol shot, I stopped dead.

Screams broke out behind me, mingling with shouts and oaths. Spinning round, the dramatic scene was etched for a moment on my mind, the audience immobile with shock, a man in the aisle pointing a gun up at the stage box I had recently occupied.

My startled glance flew to the box. Enrico was no longer visible. He must have been hit. Was he wounded or killed?

Then all hell broke loose. The stragglers still weaving their way back to their seats turned and began to dash for the entrance again, to be met by others who had just left the bar and, not knowing what had happened, were trying to force their way in. In the midst of these two forces I was caught, unable to move either way.

In the melee, the man who had caused the stampede was

engulfed and lost sight of. Then the main lights snapped on and a voice was raised from the orchestra pit, telling us all to keep clam. Everything would soon be under control. The *carabinieri* would be here directly, and in the meantime no one should leave the premises.

Only half convinced, the aisle remained thronged with people, all talking excitedly with much gesticulating in their exuberant Italian way.

What would I find on my return to the box I wondered, nerving myself to move. Then just as I emerged into the foyer, a man, head bent, looking neither to left nor right, walked swiftly past me from the auditorium and made for the exit.

The doorman stood guard, no doubt under instruction to prevent anyone from leaving. But curiously, the man leaned toward him, murmured a few words in his ear, and was allowed to go without hindrance.

And as he bent to speak, something about him and the brief glimpse I had of his profile convinced me that it was Angelo.

Excitement shot through me. So Angelo had made a bid to exterminate one of the prime enemies of his movement. Now I had a good idea why he had been allowed to slip away. The doorman was one of the resistance fighters.

Could he give me Angelo's address, I wondered with a surge of hope, for where Angelo was, surely I should find Carlo. I must be quick, before the *carabinieri* arrived, and while the doorman was still alone. Almost at a run I crossed the foyer.

"No one is allowed to leave the theater, signorina," the doorman said, barring the way.

"Oh, I've no intention of leaving. I merely wondered if you could give me the address of the gentleman you have just allowed out," I said. "It's extremely important."

A wariness came over him. "The signorina is mistaken. No one went out."

"Oh, come now!" I leaned close and whispered, "I am one of your supporters, and the password is Swordfish calling."

No flicker of recognition crossed his face. Clearly he mistrusted me and was not to be drawn.

"I think perhaps the signorina has taken a little too much chianti at the bar," he said smoothly. "Where is your escort? You are too young to be alone in such a crowd with a desperate gunman at large."

He was cool, I reflected furiously, yet only by such vigilance and staunch loyalty could such men live to fight another day.

"Return to your seat, signorina," the man urged. "Soon the *carabinieri* will arrive and you may be questioned or even arrested if you speak so strangely."

Was that a threat or a warning to hold my tongue if I really were in the confidence of the rebels? Betrayal was the last thought in my head, so when the loud honking of a motor horn and the slamming of car doors indicated the *carabinieri* arrival outside, I turned and sped away toward the staircase and Gorini's stage box.

The small enclosure when I reached it seemed to be full of people. There was Carlotta, strangely garish in stage make-up and costume, kneeling on the carpet beside Enrico. There were also several men—theater officials no doubt.

"What has happened?" I gasped, playing the wide-eyed innocent for all I was worth.

"Signore Gorini was shot at from the auditorium," the manager explained. "But the exits have been sealed and the culprit will no doubt be caught when the *carabinieri* arrive."

"How is Enrico?" I asked, sinking down beside Carlotta.

"Again, I shall live to fight another day," he said drily. "I'm too tough to be killed off easily, and before I am I mean to kill the rogue who is hounding me."

His elegant coat had been removed and a white towel was wrapped about his left shoulder. He looked pale but composed.

"Where were you at the height of the drama?" he spat out suddenly.

"I had to visit the powder room," I said glibly. "Afterward I was so thirsty I queued up at the bar for a bitter lemon. I couldn't make out what all the rumpus was about, nor easily push my way through the crowds to get back. Down below there's quite a stir."

The arrival of the *carabinieri* with a doctor put an end to private questioning. *They* now asked the questions and then prepared to help Enrico down to the waiting ambulance.

"Shall I stay here or come with you?" I asked him as Carlotta was hustled away by the stage manager to begin the next act and calm the audience, praying that he would not want me along.

"You will need a slight operation and certainly be kept in overnight," the doctor declared. "But as your injury is not serious, there is no need to subject the signorina to the ordeal of waiting around at the hospital. You can get in touch by phone with her tomorrow."

I could scarcely conceal my satisfaction until he was out of sight. Then, with the lights dimmed and the drama on stage taking over from reality, I flung my lacy stole about my shoulders and slipped away. If Carlotta noticed my absence, it would cause no speculation. She would probably conclude I was too shaken by the episode to sit on alone until the end.

Actually I cared little what she thought. To sit still with my mind in such turmoil was impossible. I just had to get outside.

Although the performance had been allowed to continue and the audience now sat in rapt attention, down below in the foyer there was plenty astir. Half a dozen *carabinieri* armed with guns were questioning the doorman, the stage manager, and several voluble ushers. I paused for a moment at the head of the broad staircase then hastily withdrew out of sight.

There was no escape that way. I should be pounced on immediately I was seen trying to leave, questioned and detained. But there must be a number of exits in a place of such size.

I began to prowl and presently came on a lighted sign. Apparently the fire exit led down from behind this hefty door, if I could only get it open.

Though heavy and stiff, a resolute push got me through to a long, dim passage, down which I sped, following the arrow signs. A second door at the end opened on to a steep flight of stone steps, and down these I went as fast as my stylish shoes would go. They seemed never ending, but stopped at last in a small bare lobby.

A bolted door now barred my way. Was it also locked? Holding my breath, I eased the bolt from its socket, and to my great relief, the door opened on to a deserted back alley.

Not quite deserted, for at the far end, in this haven from the busy main street, stood a *carrozza*, the driver singing lustily to himself in the way of the Neopolitans.

I sped toward him, then paused, staring out at the passing traffic, and the pavements lively with strolling families enjoying the cooler evening air, uncertain what to do or where to go next.

The thought of returning to the hotel held no charm. I was too concerned about Angelo, and whether he had got far enough away from the theater to be safe.

If only I could have contacted him.

The *carrozza* driver stared at me with lively interest. He ceased his singing and invited me in his florid Italian way to take a drive.

I still hesitated.

Thinking perhaps that I did not understand Italian, he tried again in passable English.

"You take the drive, signorina?"

"I don't quite know what to do now." I was thinking aloud, rather than replying to him.

Suddenly comprehension dawned in his face. Taking in my pretty dress, my distressed air, my solitary state, he nodded.

"So! You quarrel with your signore in theater. He run away in interval. Now you wish to find him and make up?"

I almost smiled at his typical Italian deduction. It seemed a logical conclusion.

He beamed. "Come, signorina, maybe I help. I saw him but a few minutes ago. He hurry past and turn right. We may yet catch him."

In a flash I saw what had happened. Angelo being directed by the doorman to some safe hiding place until the *carabinieri* had arrived and it was safe for him to show his face, then making off from this back entrance just ahead of me.

"Was he tall and broad with black curly hair?" I asked breathlessly.

"*Sì, sì!* Come!"

I was up like a flash. He flicked his whip and the horse responded. We moved out into the main road and turned right.

The horse trotted along at a smart pace, moving with the mainstream of cars, *carrozzas*, cycles, and carts. With a desperate intensity I glanced continuously first right then left, raking the pavements for any man hurrying along on his own.

Most of the pedestrians were in convivial groups, strolling and chatting, so single males stood out, but from the rear they looked confusingly alike. Twice I felt sure we had found our quarry, only to be disillusioned when we drew abreast and I saw that it was not Angelo.

Then, along the Via Cesario Console, we were halted by a smart traffic policeman to let a stream of pedestrians cross the road. Among them was a man on his own with black curly hair. The hurried glance he cast behind him showed for a moment his full face, and with a thrill of excitement I knew that it was really Angelo.

"There he is!" I gasped.

"*Sì, sì signorina*. I cannot move until I am directed, but I keep him in sight."

With a sleek car ahead of us, and the city sounds drowning my voice, I failed to attract his attention. Chafing with impatience I was forced to watch Angelo cross with the stream of pedestrians and disappear into a side street.

Even when the traffic moved forward, my driver had to wait until he could cross the road and turn off to follow. The side street gained, we found our target had placed a considerable distance between us, and then as we began to overtake him, he again turned off.

"This Santa Lucia district. Old and poor," the driver said as we followed as swiftly as we could.

High crumbling houses festooned with washing now hemmed

us in on either side, but traffic was light so there was no difficulty in keeping Angelo in sight.

Once again he turned off. Via Stromboli read the sign at the
corner when we reached it. This was a short cul-de-sac, and
within a minute Angelo disappeared into the house at the far
end.

Rather than take any risk of the driver talking, I stopped the
carrozza, paid him off with a handsome tip, and hurried along
the street alone. How dirty and neglected it was, with its broken
pavements and crumbling dwellings.

On closer inspection the last house was larger and even more
dilapidated than its neighbors. Normally, I should have been
repelled, but now I thumped the knocker without a thought
for my own safety.

There was no answer, and with slatted wooden shutters barring every window, not a light could be seen.

I knocked louder. This time a small shutter in the door slid
open disclosing a wrinkled face. In Italian, the old man asked
my business.

Haltingly I told him my name and enquired for Angelo or
Carlo, adding in a low tone, "Swordfish calling."

Without a word he drew back an inside bolt, opened the
door and let me pass inside, barring it behind me.

The hall in which we stood must have been attractive once,
with its marble mosaic floor and painted ceiling. But now the
marble was dirty and worn, and the ceiling faded. How incon-
gruous I must have looked there in my grand dress.

As though he thought the same, the doorkeeper stared curiously at me.

"We do not get many such as you here," he said at last.

"I've been to the opera," I explained. "There was a shooting
incident involving Angelo, a friend of mine, so I slipped away
and managed to follow him. I saw him enter this house a minute ago. Is his friend Carlo here too?"

The old man was still guarded. "I cannot tell you. Wait here.
I go and see what I can find out. Signorina Lisa Moravia, you
say?"

I nodded. He shuffled off up the steep creaking staircase, leaving me standing there.

After what seemed an age, down the grimy steps, at a pace which threatened disaster, bounded Carlo.

"Lisa, *mia*, what in heaven's name are you doing here! How did you find our lair? Are you certain you were not followed?" he demanded.

"Quite certain." I briefly outlined the events from that startling shot in the auditorium until now. "So you see, my finding you both was a sheer stroke of luck," I ended.

"So! Come and see him."

Arm about me, he drew me up the winding ascent to a garret on the top floor. Here I found Angelo, sprawling on a rickety couch.

"I'm glad to see you gave them the slip and are none the worse for your audacious exploit," I said.

"Never mind me. What of Gorini?" Angelo asked. "Did my bullet finish his knavish tricks once and for all?"

"Unfortunately, no. He was wounded in the shoulder but not seriously, I believe. He was taken to hospital for minor treatment. That was how I managed to get after you. Carlo will tell you about it."

"We're scarcely on speaking terms," Carlo growled. "He knows Gorini is my pigeon, then sneaks out to the opera without telling me, when he finds out that Gorini has taken a box there. It would have served him right if he'd been caught, taking such a damn fool risk. And then what of that important commission we've been given to do?" Carlo glared at the other.

"Softly, softly, my friend," Angelo said placatingly. "There is no harm done, so let us drink to the success of our mission, while Signorina Lisa can join in. We have wine and a glass or two."

But little else, I reflected, gazing round the shabby room. Silently I cursed Gorini and the Fascists for robbing Carlo of his inheritance and bringing him to such squalor.

"I'll tell you what," I burst out, suddenly longing to do something to help him. "I've plenty of money on me. Why not come

out with me, both of you, and we'll have a dinner to remember."

He thrust a glass of cheap wine into my hand. Angelo clinked
glasses and tossed his off in one gulp.

"You forget, signorina, that I'm a hunted man. I shan't stir
from here tonight," he declared. "Neither Carlo nor I show our
faces abroad if we can help it."

Carlo laughed recklessly, his dark eyes flashing with a challenge he could not resist.

"Speak for yourself, my friend. Personally, I can't resist the
offer of a decent meal and issued by so charming a signorina.
As to showing my face, I've no intention of doing so. For what
were disguises invented?"

He opened a cupboard door and whipped out a luxuriant false
moustache, which he clapped to his upper lip. It transformed
him so much I burst out laughing.

"Well now, if you make fun of me, I shall stay and eat bread
and cheese with Angelo," he threatened.

"Oh no, no! I just love your moustache. It will make the
evening quite hilarious!" I assured him.

"So! Then we shall stroll down to the waterfront of Santa
Lucia, where all the lovers go. It is quiet there after dark, and
so beautiful."

My heart lurched. A stroll in the moonlight with Carlo
sounded the nearest thing to heaven.

"You see, you do not need me at all," Angelo teased as we
set off.

"Take care, the stairs are steep and ill lit." Carlo slipped his
arm about my waist to guide me down, and kept it there when
we began to stroll along the street.

It was lovely down by the sea, where a breakwater enclosed
a calm lagoon. I shall always remember Santa Lucia in the
moonlight, with Carlo beside me.

We strolled to a more lively section and a little trattoria sent
out an inviting odor from its tables under the stars.

"They used to make good pizza there years ago," he told me.

I laughed. "Then we'll try one. I'm in funds at the moment, and ravenously hungry. Come on!"

It was still good, when it came piping hot to our table a short while later. I contrived to fill Carlo's plate with the bulk of it, and it was the merriest meal I had known for a long time.

Magic moments, but they could not last.

"What are these important plans you and Angelo are working out?" I asked when we were sipping the last of our wine.

He smiled ruefully. "You know I can't tell you that, Lisa, *mia*. But it will be of tremendous importance to our movement, and a great loss to the Fascists, if we can pull it off. Of course there are others in it besides Angelo and me."

Suddenly I was afraid for him. Whatever it was, it sounded highly dangerous.

He saw my reaction, and pressed my hand reassuringly.

"Don't fret for me. I'm a tough guy. You are in an equally precarious position, my Lisa. It turns my blood cold when I think of you out on those desolate hills, at the mercy of Gorini in the villa he's stolen from you. So far away from any protection I could give you."

I was about to put on a brave face when I remembered Margaret and Francesca, and was silent.

Reaching into an inner pocket he brought out something that gleamed in the lantern lights. Looking closer I saw that it was a small lapel decoration in the form of a swordfish.

"I've had it for years. I call it my mascot," he said. "Now I want you to take it. If ever you are in trouble and need me urgently, send it to me with the stable lad you told me about. I'll come like the wind to you."

"But it might break your luck to part with it," I protested.

He shrugged. "Keep it. Only then shall I feel a little happier about letting you go back to the wilderness. But you would be just as vulnerable staying here, without means or protection, especially when I'm no longer here. There seems no other way at the moment."

No other way. I realized it painfully as I sped toward the

hotel in the taxi Carlo had found for me. And now my only comfort was that little silver swordfish thrust into my evening bag.

Would its magic be strong enough to keep me safe?

Chapter Fifteen

It was very late when I reached the hotel, but with Gorini in hospital, who was to know and ask awkward questions.

Not surprisingly, I slept late. It was ten o'clock before I was up and dressed, and then, just as I was about to make my way to the dining room in search of a belated breakfast, to my great surprise, Gorini knocked and entered.

All I could do was stare. He looked quite himself, apart from a slight bulge beneath his sweater on his left shoulder that suggested a bandage.

"So you were not badly hurt," I stammered at last.

"Obviously not. Once again the assassins hounding me were foiled and inflicted only superficial damage. The hospital treatment was over and done with by midnight, but I was dopey from the local anaesthetic, so remained there until now."

"That's good," I said as convincingly as possible.

His face was stony.

"Oh no, my dear Lisa. You, I think owe me an explanation."

"An explanation?" My mouth was so dry I could scarcely speak.

"As to where you were until so late last night. The hospital rang you at twelve fifteen to ask you to collect me this morning. There was no answer. The receptionist said your key was still at the desk and you were out."

This was daunting, to say the least. Could quick wits and inventions save me once again?

"And don't pretend you were at Carlotta's party," he went on tersely. "When she was contacted she said you had left the theater early and had not been seen since."

"How could I sit alone for the remainder of the opera after such an episode?" I said quickly. "I just had to get away."

"To where?"

"Well, I knew it was no use returning to the hotel so early, I'd have just sat wondering how you were. I walked about for a while, then when the wolves started pestering I hailed a *carrozza* and drove for miles."

He just stared at me, his black eyes boring like gimlets, compelling me to say more.

"I ended up down at the port of Santa Lucia," I finished shakily. "It was so pleasant down there. I found an open-air trattoria and had pizza. It was very good. Finally, I took a taxi back. I didn't think it mattered staying out late as you weren't there."

The further questioning I expected never came. He only said, "If you want any breakfast make it snappy. We're taking a drive."

All I wanted was coffee. In my present state of nerves I could never have forced down food. I drank two cups, and then to my consternation Enrico insisted that I put on the blue dress I had worn to the opera, in spite of my objections that it was unsuitable for mornings.

Then we went out into the bright sunshine and boarded a waiting taxi.

"The port of Santa Lucia," he ordered.

Now I guessed his diabolical scheme. He meant to find out at source if my explanations were true or false.

The drive was an agony to me.

On reaching the waterfront he dismissed the vehicle and we took to our feet.

How beautiful it was with its rocks and bays and the sunlight shimmering on the sparkling water. This morning the rocky breakwater was lively with slim brown youths, fishing, diving, and sporting like puppies in the sea, while on a farther headland a great castle stood sentinel.

It brought an involuntary shudder, reminding me suddenly of its sinister counterpart in Almina. Enrico's hand closing over my wrist enhanced the aura of menace as he turned to walk by the sea, the way Carlo and I had gone last night.

"This area is familiar enough to me," he said. "It was one of my boyhood haunts. I know all the eating places, since I begged or stole food from them when hard pressed. The most patronized by tourists is the Bella Vista, with its open-air garden tables."

It sounded dauntingly like the one Carlo and I had chosen.

"Tell me when we reach the place you patronized," Enrico said as he marched me along.

Presently it was there, fronting the road and the sea. I could see the name clearly in the daylight. Bella Vista.

I kept walking, trying not to show recognition, but devilishly Enrico halted.

"Surely your memory plays tricks, Lisa, *mia*. This, I should guess, is where you ate that admirable pizza, if indeed you came this way at all."

I shrugged. "How can I tell? Places look quite different in half darkness."

"We shall easily find out."

He crossed the road and led me unwillingly inside, then sat down at one of the tables.

"The coffee is as good as the pizza. A cup will be welcome," he said.

A waiter ambled out. Enrico ordered, then asked if he remembered seeing me the previous evening.

The waiter shook his head. "It was my evening off, signore. Roberto served out here."

"Is he around?"

"*Si, si.* He is laying the inside tables for lunch."

"Fetch him out." Enrico passed him the open sesame of a generous tip.

"*Grazie, signore.*"

The waiter vanished, to be followed by a tubby older one who looked all too familiar to me.

"Did you serve this lady with pizza late last night?" Enrico asked. "Surely you could not forget such a pretty signorina in her attractive blue dress."

Roberto eyed me closely, then chuckled. "How could I not notice one so beautiful, signore. Such a striking couple they made. She and the so handsome young signore."

Enrico never turned a hair. He tipped the man as a matter of course and began to sip the coffee that now appeared. Dry mouthed, I followed suit.

"So," he said softly when our cups were emptied. "Are you now ready to enlarge on your little nocturnal adventure? You evidently told the truth up to a point. Now tell the rest of it. Who was your companion?"

He could kill me before I revealed Carlo's name. The only recourse was to drop my standards and invent a pick-up.

I hesitated, groping for a name. The reluctance would merely add to the probability of my reply.

"Mario," I murmured at last. "I never discovered his other name."

He just stared in that disconcerting way of his, plainly skeptical.

"Are you asking me to believe you picked him up in the street?"

"Oh, no. We happened to bump into each other at the bar in the theater," I said glibly. "He bought me a drink along with his own as I couldn't get served."

"And wanted nothing in return?"

"Of course. He wanted to meet me after the show. I told him I had an escort already, so he could expect nothing."

"Go on."

"He wasn't put off so easily. Said he was in the back row of the stalls and there was a vacant seat beside him if I cared to join him. Then came the sound of shooting and the uproar in the theater. The audience ran amok. I had a struggle to get back to our box."

"Convenient for you when you found I was the target," he said drily. "I suppose you mean to imply you joined this fellow as soon as I was taken off to hospital?"

"Soon after. I felt so alone up there in that box, the target for curious glances after what had happened."

Did he believe me? Who could tell with Enrico.

"And after the final curtain?"

"We strolled around for a while, then he suggested a snack down by the sea. Driving in a *carrozza* sounded fairly safe, so I agreed. The time flew more quickly than I realized, so I was rather late in."

"I'm surprised you weren't later."

"Oh, he didn't say *buona sera* easily. But I've a will of my own, and I insisted on the taxi dropping me at my hotel.

How maddeningly poker-faced he was. I had no clue as to whether he had swallowed my story or not. But the most important thing was, I had kept Carlo and Angelo out of it.

Or had I?

He left money on the table, and we drove back to the hotel. For the rest of the day he was absent. I mooned about miserably, spending the hot afternoon in my room, glad when it was over.

The following morning we were on our way back to Almina. A long, hot, unpleasant day of traveling that left me as limp as a rag, so that after a quick wash, on arrival, I was glad to escape into the comparatively cool grounds of the villa for a saunter before dinner.

I left myself just five minutes to change into something fresh for the meal, but when I dashed into my bedroom I stopped short in anger, for there, searching through the small case in which I kept my few most precious possessions, was Enrico.

"You have no right to spy on me!" I protested angrily. "That case was kept locked. You must have forced it open."

He turned, his own face dark with anger.

"To good purpose. I have suspected your duplicity for some time. Now I'm proved right."

In his hands he held the beautiful watch that had belonged to Carlo's mother.

Incensed, I tried to snatch it from him.

"It doesn't belong to you. You stole it in the first place!" I declared, discretion deserting me.

He laughed shortly, grasping my arm in a vicelike grip. "Now you've told me a great deal. I see *you* didn't steal it from my desk. You know too much about it. It was the masked intruder. You're in league with the fellow, beyond a doubt. That incident of finding hospital property in the cave strengthens the assumption. The audacity of it! Living under my roof and helping villains who would rob and murder me!"

I was stunned into silence. What invention could help me now?

"That faked story about picking up a Romeo at the theater doesn't deceive me either," he went on, his face too close to mine for comfort. "Strange, wasn't it, that a further attack was made on me that very evening. The assumption is you tipped the rogue off that I would be there at the time. No doubt you were both piqued that I wasn't killed instantly."

"That's not true," I protested. "I was as surprised as you by the shooting incident. How could I have been in touch with anyone before the show?"

"Easily, when you went out shopping alone."

His devastating shrewdness took my breath away. The strange thing was that I actually *had* seen Carlo, but only a glimpse of him crossing a street in the distance.

My face betrayed me.

"There, I see by your expression that you *did* have contact, so don't deny it!" he roared. "Now out with the name. Who is this man who hounds and robs me? I've not yet forgotten the loss of my valuable horse, or the attempt to burn down my plantation buildings."

"Surely you're realistic enough to realize that one man could never carry out so many raids!" I said heatedly. "No doubt there is a gang of them."

"No doubt. The question is, who is the ringleader?"

I set my teeth. Carlo's life now meant more to me than my own.

His grip on my arm tightened so that I winced with pain.

"You defy me, eh? Well, I can make a good guess. This watch clinches it. One man hates me above all others. Carlo Valachi. A fanatical member of the resistance movement. Young and devilishly good-looking as the waiter described him. *He* took you to the Bella Vista last night, didn't he?"

I was silent.

"And he was the rogue who fired at me in the theater. I might have guessed."

"You're quite wrong," I stormed. "Carlo never came near the theater."

"Then it was one of his followers. It amounts to the same thing in the end. One of these days that young vagabond and I will fight it out to the death. This world isn't big enough to hold us both, half brothers though we may be."

I stared in stupefaction. Before I could answer, the gong was heard, summoning us to dinner.

He released me abruptly. "Be down in five minutes," he said turning away. "I'll decide later what to do about you."

I shivered, rubbing the red mark on my arm. My mind was still stunned by the shock of his disclosure. Now I knew the reason for the deadly feud between this man and Carlo, and the knowledge made me more afraid than ever.

What a grim and silent meal followed. Enrico ate with his usual gusto, but I could only pick at the food, too nervous to enjoy a mouthful.

He made no objection when, on the plea of travel weariness, I escaped to my bedroom. Actually, I did feel curiously heavy and lethargic, but a morbid fear of Enrico making a sudden appearance to pronounce some devilish punishment he had thought up kept me awake until my eyelids would no longer remain open.

A black void followed in which I heard or saw nothing. Yet in the morning, when sluggishly I opened my eyes, I retained a hazy impression of someone or something moving close to me. Of a sudden prick on my right knee as though a wasp had stung me.

Oddly, my knee still felt painful and stiff. Struggling to a sitting position I threw back the single sheet to see if anything showed.

It was slightly swollen and red. Looking closer I could see a small puncture mark in the center of the inflammation.

So something *had* bitten or stung me in the night. Probably a mosquito. There were still a few around in this southern province, though they were not now malaria carriers as in former times.

And then, from a fold in the sheet, crawled a large spider. With a shudder of distaste, I flicked it from the bed and watched it scuttle into a corner. Undoubtedly this was the creature that had bitten me during the night. It was fortunate that it had not inflicted several more.

A sudden stab of pain in the knee made me wince. I had better do something about it, I decided. Some of these southern insects could cause considerable trouble.

I slid from the bed and hastily washed and dressed. The spider was still in the corner. I was just about to squash it with my sandal when I paused.

Working in the hospital had taught me that it was much easier to apply the right antidote if the exact cause of the trouble were known. If I cornered the creature, I could show it to Dr. Crossley, and it had better be soon.

I tipped some matches from a box by my candle, which was necessary because of the unreliability of electricity in these parts. Then picking up my tweezers I approached the corner and deftly transferred the spider to the box.

I now had a raging thirst. My mouth felt so dry that I made my way down to the kitchen to beg a cup of tea from Gemma, the fat cook, as it was too early for breakfast. Although the wife of Spadoni, she was quite unlike him. Her face usually wreathed in smiles, she was an easy-going and kind person.

I found her alone in the kitchen preparing a fish dish for her master's breakfast. She showed no resentment at my early intrusion and request for tea.

"*Si, si, signorina.* Sit you down. Why you limping? Have you hurt your leg?"

I nodded.

"I've been bitten by a wretched spider that crawled under my sheet during the night. It feels painful and stiff. I'll have to get some remedy up at the hospital presently."

I thrust out my knee for her inspection.

She stared, pursing her lips.

"What color spider, signorina?"

"Oh, very unusual. A mixture of orange and brown."

She raised her hands in horror.

"*Dio, mio!* Then it was a tarantula! You must go and get it seen to at once, signorina. It can be dangerous, even deadly, if neglected. I know."

I paled, feeling worse than ever now.

She poured me a cup of tea.

"Drink this, signorina, then tell the master. Maybe he take you in the car to the hospital."

"Oh, I can still manage to walk," I declared, hating the thought of meeting Enrico again. "I'll get along now if you think I'd better. You can explain what has happened to Signore Gorini."

I limped off, feeling a little better after the tea, and more so once in the fresh coolness of the early morning air.

How good it would be to see David again, to put him in the picture and hear his comforting advice on my present troubles.

A shock lay in wait. On reaching the hospital the receptionist informed me that Dr. Crossley was not there. Her doleful expression led me to ask what had happened to him.

"Alas, signorina, he was arrested yesterday evening. Two Fascist officers came and searched the hospital, accusing him of being a traitor, aiding outlaws, then took him away. Thank heaven they did not find Swordfish Ward."

This was shattering.

At my frank dismay she added, "Dr. Callas is in charge during his absence. If you wish to see him, he is in his office."

"Thanks, I do. I've been bitten by a noxious spider, but all I can think of at the moment is the dreadful news."

I sought him out. No doubt he was competent enough and would give me the correct treatment. But it was not my physical state that troubled me so much as the nervous apprehension, both for my own precarious state and now David Crossley's. Only he could appreciate the danger in which I now stood, and only to him could I have poured out the drama of the last couple of days. Dr. Callas knew none of these things, nor of the hospital's secret work. Undoubtedly Gorini was behind this arrest, I reflected in anguish.

Dr. Callas looked keenly at my knee.

"You have the spider with you, you say?"

I opened the box. He impaled the creature with a probe and examined it through a magnifying glass.

"You are lucky, signorina," he presently pronounced. "This is a tarantula, and had it been a female, you would have been very ill. Indeed, the bite often proves fatal. This one is a male, and fortunately the male's bite is less deadly."

"Well thank heaven for that," I said shakily.

"That doesn't mean it can be shrugged off as nothing," he went on, reaching for a syringe. "I'll give you an injection as well as a local application, then the best thing you can do is go home and rest. That is the speediest way to recovery."

I certainly felt groggy and the knee more painful and stiff than ever, but as for resting at the villa, that was not going to be easy in the present crisis. What would happen to David? Torture, imprisonment, execution? If only Carlo were here.

Deeply troubled, I submitted to the injection and local application.

"Shall I ring through to the villa for someone to fetch a car for you, signorina?" he asked when my knee was bound. "Walking will be difficult and painful."

I shook my head. "It's such a short distance, I'll manage all right."

"Well, come back if it gives you any further trouble, but I imagine it will gradually fade away now." With an encouraging smile he let me out.

Slowly I limped back to the villa. The immediate outlook

was bleak indeed. As bleak as Enrico's expression when I entered the dining room to find him halfway through breakfast.

"Spadoni told you about my knee?" I asked. "The spider was a tarantula. Dr. Callas says I'm lucky that it happened to be a male, otherwise it could have meant curtains for me. It's painful enough as it is, but his treatment should prevent anything worse developing."

"Dr. Callas? I'm surprised Crossley didn't rush to your assistance," he said drily, testing me out, perhaps.

"He happens to have been arrested. Surely that is not news to you!"

"So!" Was that a momentary gleam of satisfaction in his eyes? He chose to ignore my challenge, and calmly went on eating his breakfast.

Suddenly it struck me. He had expressed neither surprise nor regret at my odd mishap. Almost as though he had known all about it. Had expected a more drastic result.

Was he perhaps responsible for the incident? Had he himself placed the creature in my bed, hoping it would be the end of me and my meddling?

Everything began to fall into place like the pieces of a jigsaw puzzle. The heavy lethargy I had felt last night, coupled with my dry mouth this morning, could have been the result of a sedative drug administered at dinner.

Now, distinctly, I remembered the hazy impression of something or someone moving in my room during the night, and the quick stab of pain on my knee, before lethargy blotted both out again. How easy for Enrico to carry out his devilish plan after giving the drug time to work, and release the noxious creature on my leg.

He probably hoped the bite would prove fatal, not knowing enough about tarantulas to distinguish one sex from another. Had I died that way, no suspicion would have been directed toward him. It would simply have been attributed to an unfortunate mischance.

Now at last the peril in which I stood came fully home to me. This man had murdered in cold blood before. Each time it would come a little easier. He would have no compunction in eliminating one he considered a flagrant traitor and an increasing menace to his own safety, even if it meant an end to his designs on Nantallon Castle.

Nothing now stood between me and his ruthlessness, I realized flatly. Having failed once, he would set to work to devise another and more foolproof method of bumping me off. And neither Carlo nor David Crossley were at hand to snatch me from this perilous situation.

Glancing his way, I saw that he was regarding me with sardonic intensity. Surely he sensed the panic that was racing through me, and savored it with fiendish glee.

"You will confine yourself to the house and immediate surroundings, for your own good," he decreed. "Knowing your foolhardiness, I can't trust you to obey orders, so the main gate will be kept locked and the dog on the loose for the time being."

This was shattering. I was virtually a prisoner. Barred from making any attempt to reach the hospital again and take refuge there, even if that were practicable now that my confidant and patron had been snatched away.

He pushed back his chair and stalked from the room, leaving me to force down what food I could.

Then, steeling myself to think clearly, I remembered the tiny silver swordfish Carlo had given me. And, I remembered what he had said.

Surely I needed him now but I knew Enrico was on the alert against us both. In addition, there was the fearful anxiety over David. Carlo might possibly be able to help him, if only I could reach him and explain matters.

Yet in the present circumstances I should need help to escape. I rose painfully and limped out. I must talk to Beppo. As I emerged from the back door I was just in time to see Enrico drive off in his car. This suited me very well. I could now confer with the stable lad with no fear of being overheard or interrupted by anyone.

I found him cleaning horse brasses, his face distinctly doleful.

"Beppo, I need your help," I said.

He shrugged. "How can I help, signorina?"

"I want you to help me escape. We could escape together."

"But signorina, I have no money, and Signore Gorini would soon find and punish me."

"Not if you vanished in a big city," I said, quick to seize on the chance fate seemed to be flinging my way. "Naples, for instance, is so vast he'd never find you there."

The lad stared, not yet convinced. "But where would I go? What would I do? Work hard to get everywhere."

I leaned closer, even though I knew no one could overhear.

"Why not join the resistance movement, Beppo, and fight against such men as Gorini? Italy will never be free until the Fascists are beaten. It isn't an easy life—far from it—but you'll be free, no longer a slave, and even if you died in the cause, you'd have struck a blow for freedom."

His expression brightened. He dropped his polishing rag. "I wish I could," he said with fervor.

I grasped his shoulder. "We simply take the train. I have more than enough for both our fares. I also have an address of friends who will help us. We would both be safe from Gorini once we reached it."

He seemed eager, yet still afraid of taking such a step.

"Unless I go quickly, I shall soon be dead. That monster has already tried to kill me by means of a tarantula. It didn't act as he planned, but he'll try again very soon I'm convinced."

I showed him my knee.

"Until the poison wears off I'm partly crippled, and in addition Gorini has locked the gates to prevent any attempt at escape. Without your help I can do nothing, Beppo. You will help me, won't you?"

He looked scared, but agreed. We made plans to meet after dinner.

"I'll come to the stable, where you will have my mare saddled and ready for me. We'll slip away and catch the ten o'clock mail train to the coast. The only snags will be the dog and the locked gates."

"I fix the dog. Lock him in the stable," Beppo said.

"Better dope him first then or he may bark and raise the alarm. What about the locked gates?"

He shrugged. "I can find another way out, signorina."

"Splendid. I'll join you around nine o'clock then. Dinner is usually over by that time. That will give us ample time to reach the station before ten."

Enrico did not appear at lunch. It would have been a long and trying day for me, tied down as I was, had I not been keyed up by the prospect of the evening escape. I put a few necessities into my straw bag, then spent the rest of the day quietly in the patio, my leg on a footstool.

When the dinner gong went I had to steel myself to betray no tension to Enrico's sharp eyes. I need not have worried. He was the one full of turbulent fury when we met in the dining room.

He flung himself into his chair, his eyes smoldering.

"Those confounded rebels!" he burst out. "What do you think they've had the nerve to do now? I've just heard that last night they had the colossal audacity to blow up the magnificent new viaduct, a triumph of engineering that was to link the north with the south and would have been invaluable to the war effort. Now it's badly breached and the devil knows how long it will take to repair. *Dio, mio!* If I could get my hands on the scoundrels!"

Suddenly he glared at me.

"You wouldn't know anything of this would you, my little wolf in sheep's clothing?"

"I? Now you're being ridiculous!"

What a desperate effort it was to keep my voice normal, to disguise the effect of my madly beating pulse. For of course this must be the operation Carlo had hinted at during our last meeting. The dangerous assignment he and Angelo and a few others had gloriously pulled off.

Was he safe?

"Have they been captured?" I was impelled to ask. If so, there seemed no point in my trying to escape—not unless I could reach that house in Naples and enlist aid on dear David's behalf.

"Not yet," he spat out. "There are too many miserable peasants ready to shield them, not to mention the fishermen."

My heart leaped within me. With luck I should still feel his lips roving softly about my face again, as in those parting moments in Santa Lucia, for surely he and Angelo would make a beeline for cover and lie low until the hunt had died down.

"And that includes you," he added darkly. "I'd give a lot to hand young Carlo Valachi over to the authorities, or better still, dispose of him myself."

"You're so good at that game, aren't you?" I said furiously. "You very nearly disposed of me, but you'll never catch Carlo. Never!"

In one stride he was beside me. He lifted his hand and swiped it so savagely across my face that I staggered sideways and almost fell.

"That will teach you not to be so pert! And another thing, in case you're tempted, in spite of your lame leg and the locked gates, to try to get away and reach your hero, from now on you'll be locked in your room."

"Oh, no!"

"Oh, yes! Now sit down and get on with your soup. You'll get short shrift when it comes to Spadoni carrying trays up to the top floor, I warn you."

I forced myself to eat mechanically the thick minestrone while I reviewed the situation. What would Beppo do when I did not appear as planned? I hardly dared think.

But when, after the meal, I was bustled upstairs and the key firmly turned upon me, I was forced to face the terrifying fact that I might never leave this room alive. Even now that arch villain was probably thinking up a better way to be rid of me, without involving himself.

Once again the Villa Caterina had ensnared a victim, and I should never see my dear Carlo or David again.

Chapter Sixteen

"You will stay locked in until you tell me where I can lay hands on Carlo Valachi and his gang," Enrico had said just before he slammed the door on me. "Unless my patience gives out first, and I rid myself of you and your meddling once and for all."

I crouched on my bed, shivering in spite of the warm evening. The irony was almost too great to be borne as I pictured Beppo saddling up Seraphina and waiting patiently for me at first, then with growing uneasiness. How disappointed he would be when there was no longer time to catch the train.

It was still only a quarter to nine, but now dark in this southern latitude. I tried to read to pass the time, but found it quite impossible. Then there was nothing to do but sit hunched on my bed, only my mind seething with impractical activity.

If only the door had not been locked I could have used the window at the end of the corridor and climbed down the fire escape as Carlo had previously done. But with nothing even remotely resembling a key in my room up on the top floor, I was as trapped as a caged lion.

The minutes ticked by. Now it was ten past nine. Beppo would be growing anxious. Would he have the nerve to seek me out? He knew I occupied a room up here on the same floor as the Spadonis, and that they would not come up to bed for at least another hour.

I leaned out of my window, desperately willing him to take the chance.

The moon was up now. Down below the ground could be

clearly seen. How quiet everything was, with all the best rooms at the other side of the house. How calm and still.

Then something moved, creeping up like a shadow. Staring up with a pale face.

I leaned farther out. "Is that you, Beppo?" I hissed.

"*Si, signorina,*" he whispered back.

"Gorini has locked me in, but you must go as planned."

"I cannot go alone," he faltered.

"You must. It's your only chance, and mine. He means to kill me if I don't betray Carlo. Wait, I'll give you money."

Swiftly I thrust notes and coins into an envelope, added the silver swordfish, sealed it, and let it fall through the window. It dropped like a stone and Beppo picked it up.

Now for the address. I dare not commit it to paper in case it fell into the wrong hands. In any case, it would have been useless since the lad could not read.

"Listen carefully," I hissed. "This is where you must go when you reach Naples. Number seven, Via Stromboli, Santa Lucia. Repeat it."

He did so, and then again.

"You *must* remember it, Beppo."

"I remember."

"The password is 'Swordfish calling.'"

He repeated that twice.

"Ask for Carlo and tell him what has happened to me. Also that Dr. Crossley has been denounced by Gorini and arrested. I fear for his life. Show him the mascot inside the envelope. If he isn't there, whoever is will tell you where to get in touch with him."

Down below Beppo nodded.

"Now hurry," I said. "If you go now you have just time to reach the station without bothering with the horse. *Run!* And take care."

Again he nodded, then melted away into the shadows.

Alone again, the tense moments over, I felt weak and washed out. Now there was nothing to do but wait with as much patience as I could summon up. Traveling overnight, Beppo should reach his destination by morning, but even if he were able to contact Carlo immediately, it would be impossible for Carlo to reach here before tomorrow evening. Somehow I would have to get through tomorrow, always assuming Enrico allowed me to do so.

What would he do when Beppo was found to be missing? It was not very likely that he would connect his disappearance with me, for I had never openly shown interest in him. Hopefully, Enrico would conclude the lad had revolted against his harsh treatment and run away.

Surprisingly, I slept well, and ate the meager breakfast that Spadoni thrust in on me. Had they discovered Beppo's absence yet?

Then opening my window wide, I sat in the fresh morning air and forced myself to calmly read an Agatha Christie mystery that had been lying untouched ever since my arrival.

By lunch time I had finished it, and inactivity was beginning to pall. When Spadoni appeared with spaghetti and ice cream I demanded to be let out for exercise, but he only grunted and slammed and locked the door.

I was both glad and apprehensive when Enrico himself glanced in after his own lunch. He was scowling blackly and looked in no mood for leniency.

"Have you come to your senses yet?" he snapped.

"I've nothing to say," I declared.

"So. We shall see what a little more solitary confinement will do. But I warn you, my patience will last only until tonight. After dinner I shall come up here once more. If you still refuse to give me information regarding Carlo Valachi, then you will go the same way as that tattling laundry maid."

Shot and thrown into the desolate ravine, where my body might lie until picked clean by birds of prey, I thought with a shudder. My habit of wandering the hillsides was known. Any enquiry would conclude that I had lost my footing and slid over some precipice to my death.

"Another rebel who will receive no mercy when caught is that worthless Beppo," he said, preparing to go. "He can't be found.

Run off with some idea of joining the rebels, I'll be bound. I'm off to search for him now, and then he'll wish he'd never been born."

It was some consolation to know that Beppo must now be beyond his reach, but my own situation was desperate, I realized with cold fear. Could Carlo reach me in time? If he were not at the Santa Lucia house, and had to be sought out, my position seemed hopeless.

The afternoon dragged interminably. I lay on my bed resting my leg, glad that it was a great deal better in case I was called upon to use it vigorously tonight. Through my mind flitted various wild plans for escape, ranging from knotted sheets to coshing Enrico smartly over the head when he appeared later, if anything heavy enough was at hand.

They were all quite impossible. In this climate my bed had only a top and bottom small sheet, totally inadequate to escape from such a height. Overpowering Enrico was equally hopeless. Like a gazelle trying to fell an ox. There seemed nothing I could do to help myself.

Spadoni at length appeared with a tray, a little earlier than the normal dinner time. Evidently getting my needs out of the way before he busied himself with the master. Had he been a more friendly character I might have made a desperate plea for his help, but I knew the futility of that.

The meal looked appetizing. A last concession to the prisoner in the condemned cell, I reflected wryly. I did not really want it, but disciplined myself to eat, saving only the half bottle of wine in the forlorn hope that if Carlo did turn up he might be desperately thirsty.

After that I opened my window wide, regardless of stray mosquitos, and sat watching and listening for the slightest sound that might indicate his approach. Unfortunately, tonight the sky was overcast so there would be little help from the moon. What a blessing Carlo had been forced to hide in my room on his last dramatic appearance at the villa and, with his splendid sense of direction, would without doubt locate it from outside.

I pictured Enrico's every move. At eight, he would be sitting down to dinner, enjoying the food as he always did. Perhaps all the more for thinking of his coming confrontation with me and just what he would do to make me betray Carlo.

Soon, so soon now, I should hear his heavy tread in the corridor and the unlocking of the door that would signal my doom, because then it would be too late for Carlo to save me. Perhaps he would walk into the trap himself, and the arch villain would have the satisfaction of ridding himself of us both together.

"Oh, God," I murmured wildly, "let Carlo come. Let him be in time."

As if in answer to the prayer, there he was below. In the poor light I could just make him out, staring up at me.

"Thank God you're still alive, Lisa," he murmured. "I had to wait until he was at dinner."

"Not for much longer. He'll be up here soon. We must be quick," I urged.

"I'll climb up the fire escape. Is the corridor window fastened inside?"

"Yes, worse luck."

"No matter. The frame's quite rotten. I'll break it."

"Take care about the noise," I cautioned as he turned away.

Helpless, I waited in an agony of apprehension. He would also have to force my door. Thank heaven for this back top-floor room, so far from the principal rooms, I reflected. With fingers that shook I pulled on my coat and picked up the straw bag.

Presently I heard someone outside. Was it Carlo, or was it— Enrico?

The fumbling at the keyhole confirmed that it was Carlo. Then the lock clicked, the door opened and he was with me, hugging me close.

"Thank heaven I had the presence of mind to bring along a master key," he whispered. "I nearly went crazy when Beppo turned up this morning and I heard of your plight. I'd not long been back from blowing up that viaduct."

"Tell me later. Come quickly before Enrico comes up," I urged.

We sped down the corridor. The window stood wide open. Carlo was just about to help me through onto the fire escape when a break in the clouds gave sufficient light to show the ground quite clearly.

My face drained of color, for there at the foot of the iron staircase stood the dog, his lips drawn back in a snarl.

"If he barks, we're cornered," I croaked. "Both Spadoni and Enrico will be out in a flash."

"Let me go first," Carlo said grimly. "I'll deal with the brute."

With baited breath I watched him descend, praying that the dog would not break out into excited barks. Mercifully, the beast considered himself quite equal to dealing with this intruder, and just stood there waiting to pounce. His snarl became a menacing growl.

Carlo, seasoned campaigner that he was, proved his equal. A foot from the dog's reach he sprang, bringing the butt of his gun smartly down on the bristling skull. With a smothered yelp the brute fell and lay still.

"Quickly, Lisa! He's only stunned, I think," Carlo urged.

I needed no prompting. Quick as a flash I was down, and hand in hand we were racing round to the front gates.

The great iron barriers stood shut, but with his magical key Carlo unlocked the small side gate. We raced through and out onto the road.

"My disappearance is bound to be discovered soon," I panted. "Even if the dog doesn't give us away, Enrico will find me gone when he goes up."

"Then he'll put two and two together and come searching for us both. Almost certainly by car. That means the road's out. We must stick to the hills for the time being. I know them pretty well."

"You came by train I suppose," I said as we set off.

He nodded. "Unfortunately that easy mode of reaching the coast is out now. Gorini will alert all the intermediate stations as soon as he realizes I'm in the vicinity. I'm now well and truly between the devil and the deep sea, Lisa, *mia*, with the Fascists out to get me and Angelo for blowing up the viaduct, and Gorini at this end. Angelo's reasonably safe lying low in Santa Lucia, but I daren't put the secret hideout at risk by trying to get back there now."

"Where shall we go?" I tried to keep my voice undismayed.

"There's a small volcanic island near the coast south of Paola. Rocky and bleak on the landward side, but with a tiny fishing village on the seaward side. They make a living spearing swordfish and are staunchly sympathetic to our cause. Many a fugitive has reason to bless them for food and shelter. If we can reach Isola Piccola unseen we should be safe."

"On foot?" I gasped. "It will take us ages."

"There are ways and means of acquiring aid," he said. "I noticed some horses grazing in an enclosure as I came up from the station. One of those will do for a start. We have to get off the road before pursuit begins."

"I remember the place. There's a wooden shed where harness is kept," I volunteered. "I've seen the door open. Your magic key should unlock it."

It was halfway down the hill. The bony horses were dozing on their feet. Carlo carefully flicked his torch over them and singled out the most likely looking beast, then picked the lock of the shed without effort.

"Needs must when the devil drives. This will compensate the owner." He placed some lire notes on the bench, seized a saddle and set to work, while I began on the bridling.

The horse was docile enough and soon we were mounted.

"We shan't get far with a double load, but well away from here at least," he said as he turned the horse away from the now potentially dangerous road and town, into a bridle path.

"You haven't yet told me what sparked off your crisis with Gorini," Carlo said as we jogged along.

"He's been suspicious of me for some time. Last night he searched my room and found the watch you gave me. Then, of course, he guessed the masked intruder was you and that I was in league with you. He said if I didn't betray your bolt hole, he'd kill me. He meant it, too. If Beppo had not been able to contact you immediately at the Santa Lucia house . . ." I broke off, shuddering, and finally mentioned the spider episode.

"Don't fret, Lisa, *mia*," Carlo promised. "One day I shall get even with him, and reclaim the watch. For the moment, the unfortunate Dr. Crossley is in the greatest danger. Bad news indeed. So-called traitors are often shot without trial now that we're at war. Time is not on his side, I fear."

My heart sank. "I feel somehow guilty," I sighed.

"Not so. We rebels face death every moment of our lives," he said somberly.

I soon lost all sense of direction, but in spite of the poor visibility because of clouds that frequently obscured the moon, Carlo went steadily on, urging the horse to its limits.

When at length it refused to go farther, and we ourselves were saddle weary, we halted and turned it loose.

It was still quite dark and some time yet to the early dawn, I realized, glancing at my luminous watch. What we needed was rest, but where?

A field of newly mown hay provided the answer. Some of the coarse grass was festooned round poles to dry off in the manner of the region, but there was still plenty lying about. We found a heap and sat down.

"I'd give a lot for a drink," Carlo sighed.

It was then I joyfully recalled the half bottle of wine saved from dinner and now nestling in the bag I still clutched.

"You shall have it, my knight errant," I promised, opening up the bag.

It tasted heavenly. Afterward we burrowed into the sweet-smelling hay and clasped in each other's arms, slept like tired children for a brief while. The first and possibly the only time I should ever lie with Carlo.

A cock crowing roused us. We rose, stretched, and shivered in the early morning hill mist. Through it, a little below us, we could see a tiny village nestling in a hollow, a few scattered farms surrounding it. Beyond and all around us stretched the rolling hills. I felt immeasurably cut off.

"Any chance of breakfast I wonder?" I pictured a Welsh frying pan filled with sizzling bacon and eggs, unlikely though it was here.

"That and more I hope, with a little ingenuity. Have you a peasant scarf in that bag of yours?"

I produced it. He tied it on, then roughed up his already tousled hair.

"We'll act a peasant couple trudging down to the coast to find work," he said. "Leave the talking to me. I'll pretend you're deaf. But you must get rid of that smart coat. Without it you look Italian enough, as indeed you are."

I slipped it off. It would, in any case, soon be too warm to need a coat. Then I deliberately tore my dress at the hem, and disheveled and grubby, we made our way to the nearest farm, thrusting the coat into a dense patch of undergrowth as we went.

The farm wife was outside milking goats as we approached. Carlo spoke to her, thrusting money at her.

She waved it away and drew us toward the dwelling, a tumbled-down little place with red roof and peeling plaster walls.

We cared nothing for this. Our eyes were on the coffeepot nestling on the charcoal brazier outside the house and sending forth an appetizing aroma.

The young girl tending it glanced up with startled scrutiny. Then at a word from her mother she carried it indoors and set it on the table. The mother motioned us to sit down, while explaining us away to her husband, already seated.

The food was plain but adequate. Coarse dark bread in great chunks, a lump of goat's-milk butter, a wedge of sharp cheese. After an exchange of words between Carlo and the man, we tucked in heartily enough after our night in the mountain air.

When it was over, the woman and girl went off about their work, while the man lingered to speak to Carlo. Presently he, too, rose.

"We're in luck," Carlo murmured when the man left us alone. "I asked about transport. There is only one bus a week into the nearest town, but as it happens, the farmer has a litter of pigs ready for sale. He's taking them into town ready for tomorrow's market. He says we're welcome to ride with him, and as it's on the rail track we should get a train down to the coast from there."

"How marvelous! When is he leaving?"

"In five minutes."

We went outside. The half-grown pigs, with much squealing and grunting, were being driven up a ramp into a high-sided truck. This was evidently one of the more prosperous farmers. Most of them possessed nothing more ambitious than bony horses and rough carts.

Even this was far from luxurious I realized as I climbed into the cab and sank down on the hard seat. But welcome indeed if it helped us on our hazardous way.

Carlo sat in the middle the better to talk to the driver, and we began our rattling, jolting ride over atrocious stony tracks, full of potholes and hair-pin bends. All around stretched the rolling hills, here and there rising to rocky peaks or falling sharply into deep gorges. Beyond an occasional straggling village or a hill shepherd with his flock there was no sign of human habitation. Only the yellow broom, bright golden in the morning sun, when the vapory clouds did not envelop us.

On reaching the town we slipped away to the tumbled-down little station, fearful of being recognized as strangers. Carlo's enquiries elicited the information that a train left for Paola on the coast in half an hour. Until it made its appearance we sat in the most unobtrusive corner of the waiting room, sipping bottled mineral water.

Although pretty full when it steamed noisily in, we squeezed into a corner of a hard wooden bench and sat silently so as not to draw attention to ourselves with my English speech. Only when we halted at the occasional station and our fellow travelers streamed out could we safely exchange a few remarks.

"Things will be hazardous when we reach Paola," Carlo confided on one of these breaks. "The bridge we destroyed was not far from there, so there's almost certain to be a watch at the station exit. Our best plan seems to be to alight at the previous station and cut across country to the south, heading toward the island."

"How long is that likely to take?"

"The rest of the day, but that suits me well enough. Getting across to the island will need the cover of darkness, as will filching a boat to transport us there."

It all sounded unnerving, but with Carlo beside me, nothing really daunted me.

A broken-down station, sizzling in the now vertical sun, was the signal for us to alight. Instead of following the few stragglers to the exit, Carlo drew me the opposite way, where we slipped out unseen through a tangle of bushes and set off along a rough path.

Away on our right gleamed the sea. Carlo consulted a map he carried and said, "There's a river running down to the sea about a kilometer away. We'll follow that. At this time of year the bed should be dried out and make a passable road. Best foot forward, Lisa, *mia.*"

He was right about the river. It was now a dry and gravelly sunken track, leading a gently winding course to the coast. Pleased with our luck in not having to pick our way across wild country, we took to this and slogged on.

The heat was now intense. We stripped off and carried our sweaters, but perspiration still bathed us as we went doggedly forward, meeting no one and seeing only an occasional cluster of mean hovels straggling down to the watercourse.

By sundown, utterly weary and parched to cinders, our flagging progress halted at a village bigger than most and offering hope of refreshment. My knee was now growing painful, though I forbore to complain.

"We're not far from the coast now, and at the mouth of this river a fishing village is marked," Carlo said, consulting his map. "If we rest awhile here, then follow this track again, we should be able to filch a boat in the darkness and cross to the island."

I nodded. Disheveled and covered in gray dust as we now were, we looked sufficiently like the locals to warrant not even a second glance. So we turned off up the straggling main street until we reached a piazza with a dingy trattoria outside which sat the usual collection of rough-clothed men sipping wine and gossiping.

We took a vacant bench on the fringe, ordered wine and pasta, and spun out the next hour in blissfully restoring our vitality. Then, feeling renewed, we returned to the river track and pushed on.

Now the moon came out, a real piece of luck. In its pale light, the white fishermen's dwellings and the tiny harbor looked remote and unearthly when we presently emerged at the coast. The few boats and fishing nets drawn up on the crescent of sand were fortunately deserted, their owners relaxing after their day's toil.

Carlo cast a calculating glance at the enclosing arm of the stone jetty. There, two or three small boats were anchored, bobbing lazily on the gentle swell.

"One of those for us I think," he murmured, leading the way. Following along the jetty I stared out to sea.

A single light here and there indicated a swordfish boat, but of the island there was no glimpse.

"It's uninhabited on this side, and high rocks in the center cut off the few cottages on the seaward side," Carlo explained.

We selected the smallest boat, cast off, and he began to row us out to sea.

"How can you locate it without lights to guide you?" I asked. He shrugged. "I know the direction. So we just go carefully and keep a sharp lookout until we hit upon it. There's an ancient ruin. Used to be a fort I believe. We should see the outline of that."

Keyed up, I strained my eyes ahead into the darkness.

After what seemed ages, a dark bulk loomed ahead.

"This is the island," I murmured, "but I can't see any building. And the cliffs seem too steep to land."

"Then we'll row parallel until we reach a tiny cove below the ruin. It's the only place one can land on this side."

"Wouldn't it be easier to row round to the fishing village on the seaward side if the island is small," I suggested, "rather than having to cross over those high center rocks?"

He shook his head. "Too dangerous. The village is already under suspicion of aiding our movement. We always approach it by this back way, for their protection and ours. We never know when a motor launch of Fascists might be snooping around out there."

Suddenly we were abreast of the cove. We climbed out, left the boat to drift and plodded across the sand to where rocks sprang up again topped by the dark bulk of broken walls.

"We skirt the ruins. From the other side a path runs across to the village, avoiding the worst peaks. We follow it to food and shelter and eventual escape to Sicily," Carlo said. "I have instructions to lie low in Sicily and await further orders."

In the hushed darkness Carlo's boots crunched noisily on the loose stones of the track winding its way round the broken fort. For some reason the sound made me uneasy. Then suddenly from the dark wall beside us a rough door was flung open and a lantern thrust into our faces, blinding us in contrast to the darkness.

"By all the saints! It's Carlo Valachi!" a triumphant voice exclaimed. "Walked straight into our trap. The arch traitor himself! Signore Gorini has first claim on him. Take him alive comrades."

Rough hands seized us. There seemed to be four of them, but with the strength of desperation, Carlo smashed his fist into the nearest face, then kicked out with his hefty boots. The lantern fell shattered to the stones and went out, while the wielder doubled up with a grunt of pain. In the confusion, Carlo succeeded in freeing me, and we ran off along the track by the ruins.

Curses, exclamations, and finally the sound of heavy boots

crunching on the stones behind us proved that we were being followed by at least two of them. Leaving the ruin behind, Carlo dived from the track in among the boulders.

"Follow me, Lisa. Keep close or you'll lose me in the poor light. We'll try to shake them off," he whispered.

There followed a grim game of hide and seek. Terrified, I ran with a speed and dexterity I never knew I possessed, as I followed Carlo, winding in and out among the rocks, ever rising to the center heights. The pain of my knee was excruciating, but I just had to grit my teeth and bear it.

Behind us the pursuit continued. A new lantern must have been brought, for its light flashed out now and again, giving away their position, but not succeeding in locating us with its limited range.

Panting and sweating we reached the peak. Now, well below, on the seaward side, we could make out the few lights of the harbor and village.

"We'll make for those," whispered Carlo. "We may get away in a boat without involving any of the fishermen. It isn't all that far to Sicily. *Avanti!*"

The descent was not going to allow us much cover, we realized as soon as our pursuers reached the crest of the hill. With the moon playing hide and seek among the clouds, for brief periods it was light enough for them to sense our movements below, when a hail of bullets would follow.

"They must be Gorini's men," I whispered during one of these moonlight spells while we crouched behind a rock. "They mentioned his name."

"He could be with them. They're blackshirts, Fascists," Carlo said. "They are after me for blowing up the viaduct. A party of them must have been sent out here on the chance that I would try to escape this way. Gorini evidently had the same idea. He realized who rescued you last night, and has made haste to the coast today. He could be anywhere in the vicinity. They are all in league together."

Our pursuers, taking advantage of the moonlight, were closer now. Passing clouds gave us a break. We melted into the shadows, stealing between the rocks, steadily descending to our goal of escape, whenever we got the chance.

Moving as swiftly and silently as possible, we at last reached level ground near the huddle of cottages. They and the minute harbor lay silent and deserted in the dim light, while above us the sounds of our pursuers suggested we had outdistanced them a little.

"Full speed ahead, Lisa, *mia*, down to the end of the jetty," Carlo urged. "We'll take the first boat we chance on."

Our sprint did not go unnoticed from above on the bare expanse of the jetty. Shouts told us they were hot on our trail.

Only two rowing boats were moored at the end.

"Jump in!" Carlo unhitched the first we reached. "It might serve to get us away. We'll make for the light of a fishing vessel. The swordfishermen will help us without question."

He leaped in after me, seized the oars and began to row strongly away on the luminous swell.

Shortly afterwards, a spatter of bullets were fired at us from the jetty.

"They'll probably have an outboard motorboat inside the harbor and come after us with that," Carlo said grimly. "Thank heaven there's the light of a fishing boat not too far ahead."

"Two lights," I said, peering out. "Keep going. You're steering in the right direction."

But gallant though his efforts were, they could not possibly compete with a motorboat. Soon the roar of an engine behind us confirmed that only a miracle could save us from capture.

The moon chose this moment to escape from the clouds, lighting up our small craft and the larger motorboat that hounded us. Instantly, there was a lionlike roar from the latter, and a voice we both recognized came bellowing over the water.

"Surrender, damn you, Valachi, unless you want the girl shot as well! You can't escape in that cockleshell! You'll both go the same way as that traitor Crossley."

"Gorini!" I groaned, "and oh Carlo, they've killed David!"

I blanched, holding my breath. The next moment a gun fired, and a bullet came straight for Carlo.

Horrified, I expected to see him fall back, dying. Instead he shipped his oars, whipped out his own gun and sat waiting until the pursuing boat closed sufficiently for his purpose.

Now we could clearly see the burly shape of Gorini peering over the side. With grim deliberation Carlo took aim and fired.

"That to avenge all your cold-blooded murders, not the least of which was a brave doctor, you wretch!" he called.

His marksmanship was superb. The swaggering figure fell from sight.

"End of a tyrant!" Carlo said somberly.

I guessed his feelings, but did not tell him I knew the truth. Let it die with Gorini.

"I can't think how *you* escaped," I said shakily. "I could have sworn I heard a ping as his bullet struck you."

Glancing down, Carlo fingered the large button on his undone tunic.

"Saved by a button!" he explained. "The bullet was deflected and passed harmlessly through the cloth under my arm, I suspect."

Gorini's sudden end had caused commotion on the motorboat. For a few moments its progress faltered, then it came at us again.

Suddenly I noticed the lights of the two swordfish boats amazingly close. Sensing trouble, they had raced up unnoticed to our aid.

"By heaven! We still have a sporting chance of escaping capture!" Carlo gasped. "They're cutting in between us and our pursuers!"

At the same time the Fascists noticed the danger.

"Change course, you fools!" they roared at the fishing vessels. When there was no response, they were forced to abruptly alter their own course to avoid collision.

The swordfishermen had no intention of letting the Fascists escape. Within seconds their two boats had separated and were converging on the enemy. There came a splintering crash as their two heavy prows caught the Fascist boat between them.

Then the fearsome yells of the men in the speed boat could be heard.

Cheering, the swordfishermen drew away and watched as the crippled boat slowly sank with her crew. Silently, Carlo and I watched too.

"Exit Gorini," I said shakily. "Now we are both free of him. If only we could say the same for David."

Carlo shook his head. "One of the unlucky ones, but he has been avenged. Now you can go back to your rightful inheritance in safety, Lisa, *mia*, while I finish off a few more tyrants. Only when Italy is free again can I relax and indulge in the pleasures of normal life. Then my love—"

"Oh, Carlo, when will that be?"

"Some day, never fear. In the meantime, maybe we have a few days together in Sicily."

"Oh, Carlo!" I murmured again as he put his arms around me and kissed me gently.